Written by Claudia Blood
Cover design by Sunset Rose Books

Copyright 2021 by Claudia Blood

Paperback ISBN: 978-1-954603-42-4

THORN OF THE ROSE

THE MERGES SERIES
BOOK 2

CLAUDIA BLOOD

DRAGON BANE PUBLISHING

With the town magic gone awry, one undead woman must uncover the truth before it kills them all...

Rose Callahand's life is full of secrets—including her own past.

Now her hometown of Hope—spared from the cataclysmic Merge three hundred years ago by four wizards—is in peril.

The magic that protects it under a shield is warping, harming those it was meant to
protect.

Rose is entrusted with a magical necklace, which if reunited with its sister necklace
on the other side of the shield would remove the protective barrier and banish the twisted magic.

Her mission fails, the necklace lost, but her memories are unlocked, bringing to light a staggering secret—Rose is undead.

With someone working against her and her friends on their quest to save the city, Rose must discover the hidden truths and unravel the twisted magic threatening everyone.

Or "die" trying...

Thorn of the Rose is the standalone, second book in the thrilling Merged Series. Fall into a world of magic and mortals and unlock the secrets people have died to keep hidden...

Trigger warning:

This book contains death, violence, and self-defense that ends in death.

1

ROSE

Rose Callahand opened her eyes. The shield protecting the town of Hope glimmered like a soap bubble. She'd made it through. Relief filled her chest with warmth. Her mission still had a chance.

She didn't remember actually crossing the shield. Her last memory was touching the shield at high sun, but now the dew on the grass and the first hint of light made everything seem gray. Had it taken all afternoon and night to cross? She shivered. The trees loomed above her. Nothing moved. The silence weighed her down.

Mistress Yaneli had determined that the shield was corrupted and was the reason for the sicknesses running rampant through Hope. Rose's mission seemed simple: take the stone necklace with the fire symbol to the man who would be waiting for her outside of the shield. Giving him the stone would allow him to break the shield around Hope.

Rose got to her knees and touched her neck where the stone should be.

There was no necklace.

Panic added a beat to her heart. Had she lost it? She slapped at her pockets. Nothing. Without it, her mission was a failure and her girls were in danger. Fear and failure crept up her back. The panic doubled.

No, she couldn't have failed.

The silver stone had been on a piece of twine. Perhaps the twine had broken in the crossing. She scanned the ground near her and saw a glimmer of gold. A different necklace with a thin gold chain and a locket sat in the grass. It wasn't what she was looking for, but she picked it up anyway.

The necklace stung her finger. Pain radiated up her hand, making it clench on the chain. The pain passed after a moment, leaving her dizzy. Someone else must have lost this necklace; she could try to return it.

Rose put on the chain. A strong urge to open the locket tightened her fingers. She ran her fingertip along the seam. The urge she felt was unnatural in its strength. The mission was more important than what was inside the locket. She would look inside later after looking for the stone necklace.

She dropped the locket, and when it hit her chest, a sudden foreboding struck her along with the sense that once she opened the locket, she would never be able to put back what she released into the world. This was her Pandora's Box. She shook her head to dispel the feeling. The mission and her girls were more important.

As she searched more ground around her, she resisted the urge to look inside the locket. But the necklace warmed against her chest and pulled at her imagination. What would be within it? Could it help her find the stone and salvage her mission? Could it help her protect her girls from Mistress Yaneli?

The last thought brought her up short. There was much she would risk, including this mission for Mistress Yaneli, to protect her daughters.

Finally, she opened the locket, revealing a photo of her two daughters grinning at the camera with their brown hair curling around their faces. She didn't remember taking such a picture. On the other side was engraved, "So we can see those we have lost". The dizziness returned, her chest burned, and she leaned heavily on one arm.

Suddenly, the knowledge that her daughters were dead hit her in the heart. *My girls are dead.* Loss, sadness, and regret throttled her heart, squeezing it until she couldn't breathe.

Hope had killed her girls. She was sure of that. The thought echoed in her head and fear rose from her burning chest. Overwhelming, crushing fear brought tears to her eyes and blurred the world. She had to get away from Hope and never go back.

Rose stumbled to her feet, gasping for breath. The smell of the loam with its hint of decayed leaves filled her nose.

Hope was behind her, so she scrambled forward.

She stumbled, landing hard against a tree. The bark was rough against her fingers. Her breath caught in her lungs, producing short, choppy sobs in her throat.

She pushed forward blindly, tripping over something, then she toppled. The ground rushed up to meet her. Dirt dusted her mouth and pain lanced her hands and knees. She had to keep moving. The desperate urge to distance herself from Hope spurred her forward.

Rose crawled.

The sound of her own breathing echoed in her ears. She crawled until the ground gave way in front of her, and she tumbled forward and landed hard. The fear loosened its hold on her chest, but it still stalked too close.

She took a pull of cool air and worked to calm herself.

A crunch sounded next to her. She opened her eyes to a pair of boots. Crouched next to her was a young man with scars covering his face. The man tilted his head, evaluating her with eyes that seemed far older than his young appearance. "Are you okay?"

She nodded even though she wasn't sure if it was true. The fear was still there in the back of her mind. It was smaller and more manageable. But the sense of grief from losing her girls still weighed her down. She tucked the necklace under her shirt and tried to focus on survival. She couldn't go back to Hope. Even thinking the town's name brought the fear closer.

"Need help standing?" His gaze traveled from her skinned knees to her nose and eyes. His scarred face twisted with sympathy. He had the look of a man who was distressed by a crying woman.

"At some point." She lifted her chin even as the tears fell down her cheeks. She didn't feel threatened by him, but the wretched sadness that crawled up her back made her glad she wasn't alone.

He handed her a handkerchief and looked away, giving her some privacy.

She blotted her face and then blew her nose, taking her time to evaluate him. Everything said that this man could be trusted. She took a breath and worked to lock down her feelings. It had been a long time since she'd been this out of control.

"I'm Joshua Lighthouse," he said as he sat next to her on the ground. He dug into his pack. He pulled out something wrapped in leather and offered it to her.

The food smelled of strange spices and it made her mouth water. How long had it been since she'd eaten? She took the food. "Thank you."

She took a bite and focused on the spice. Since she had

failed her mission and didn't want to go back to Hope, she needed a place to stay and a job. "Is there a town nearby?"

She'd already decided that there must be. Joshua didn't look like a farmer or a huntsman.

"New Nadezhda is near." His brow furrowed, but he didn't ask her where she was from.

"What sort of skills do they value there?" she asked. Since she was one of the few non-magical people from Ho—her home-town. If this new town only valued magic, she could be in trouble.

He shrugged. "What are you good at?"

"I know Hapkido." Seeing his blank expression, she added, "It's a fighting style."

He nodded, looking thoughtful. "I could use some back-up on what I'm currently working on."

Rose evaluated his face. She'd always had a sense for knowing when people were lying. Joshua was not lying. He could use the help. She didn't have many options, and he had been kind. Perhaps she could prove she was more than a sobbing woman.

"What do we need to do?" she asked.

"There is a vampire near here who has been killing in the city. I'm here to persuade him to stop." Joshua said it calmly, like it was a normal day for him to walk into a vampire's lair.

She studied his expression and the way he held himself. He acted as if he believed vampires were real.

"Do vampires really exist?"

Joshua nodded. "They do."

She thought about everything she had seen and heard about the myth of vampires. "So, he's undead, and only a stake through the heart can stop him?"

"There are other ways, but that's the most reliable one. I also have this." He pulled out a vial. "This has holy water and other things and will harm the undead." He tucked the bottle back into his bag.

Even though he seemed to be telling the truth, she still thought he must be joking. There was no such thing as a vampire. Was there?

His face and everything about him supported his words. The shield had been put up to protect Hope hundreds of years ago. Could it have been used to prevent things like vampires from entering Hope? Was that what Hope's founders had seen, what caused them to put up a wall? Why hadn't New Nadezhda put up a shield?

"I'll go, but I have questions."

"Shoot." He led her along a path near the edge of the woods.

How else was this world like Hope? "Are there many mages in the city?"

"Some. Mages are relatively rare."

Hope was full of mages. She and Max had been two of only a handful of people without magic. "And are there many creatures like the vampire here?"

Joshua raised an eyebrow at her. "Yes, there are many types of undead. Most are not intelligent. Vampires are." His tone had stayed even, but something about the slight downward curve of his mouth made her think Joshua didn't like the undead.

"Are there other things?"

"All the creatures from Earth came into this world with the Merge." His face twisted as if he was remembering something unpleasant.

She followed Joshua, barely keeping track of where they were going.

The shield had protected Hope from the Merge. She would have to get used to many different creatures. She hadn't read much about fairytales. That had been more Max and her husband's thing. The ache of grief closed her throat for a moment. She forced the emotions away.

"We're here," Joshua whispered.

A small tower, perhaps two stories high, squatted in a clearing. It didn't seem to have any windows. But that made sense. Didn't vampires have an issue with the sun? The surrounding vegetation looked like it belonged in a fairytale, dark and twisted and full of thorns.

"One of the agents at the Human Protection Agency, the HPA, swears he got in a killing blow when he rescued the woman the vampire was trying to kill." He turned back to look at her. "Sorry, I had forgotten you were without a weapon." He handed her a long dagger.

She took it, did a practice swing, and assumed her first stance. The dagger was a few inches shorter than the sword she had trained with, but would work.

Joshua grinned at her. "Ready?"

She nodded.

At Joshua's touch, the door creaked open. The smell of decay tickled her nose.

Joshua lit a torch. The room seemed to be the full length of the tower. A staircase extended down into murky darkness and up to the next level.

The smell of decay was stronger up here. "Which way?" she whispered.

Joshua pointed down.

The first stirring of unease hit her. She knew what he was hunting was upstairs, but perhaps he had a reason to go down? She wasn't sure, so she kept quiet.

Rose crept behind him, trying to make no sound.

"*Why are you with the human?*" The voice in her head sounded male and old.

Her heart picked up speed. She'd never heard a voice in her head before.

Something pungent clogged her nose. The sense she and Joshua were heading into a trap pressed on her chest. She grabbed Joshua's shoulder.

He stopped and glanced back. "What's wrong?"

"The vampire is upstairs..." She wasn't sure how to explain that going down was a trap or that she knew the vampire was upstairs. But she did. She was confident in her conclusions.

He glanced down for a moment. His breathing changed, and then all the color left his face. He took a shuddery breath. "Go back," he mouthed.

She went back up the stairs, and then Joshua led again, going up to the second floor.

The room was almost as dark as the room below, which made sense if there were no windows. It would be like a big cave.

A massive bed was just visible in the gloom. The decaying smell came from the bed.

Joshua lit a torch and brought it to the bed. The man who lay in the bed was desiccated. Dry skin stretched across his bones. A gaping wound lay open on his chest, but the wound didn't bleed.

"Lighthouse. Come to put me out of my misery?" the man hissed.

"If you agreed to not harm humans, I'd have no issue with you."

"You wish me to starve." The man leapt out of the bed, flying toward Joshua.

Joshua's first arrow hit the vampire in the throat, but the second went wide. It was enough. The vampire slowly disintegrated.

"He will kill you, too, when he finds out." The old male voice reverberated in her head. It must have been the vampire.

The words in her head confused her. Why would Joshua kill her? She wasn't undead.

She retrieved the arrow that had misfired. The shaft was sticky. She touched it and pain shot through her fingertip. She dropped the arrow. "You have poison arrows?"

Joshua raised the torch to look around the room. "Don't worry. It only affects the undead."

Rose's stomach dropped. "What do you mean?" She glanced at her fingers, which still stung.

Joshua picked up the arrow. "The potion I showed you earlier. Only affects undead. In fact, I can use it to heal myself." He touched the sticky part to a slight cut he had on his arm, and the cut healed.

Rose's heart thudded. If Joshua was right, that would make her an undead. Confusion and panic made the words stick in her throat.

"Come on. The thing in the basement should be weaker now that its master is dead." Joshua walked down the stairs.

Rose hesitated. The room should be dark with Joshua and his torch downstairs, and yet she could see the room as if it held dim light. She had smelled the vampire and he had known she was undead. She had no idea how she had become undead. Chills raced up her back and down her arms. She looked at her fingertips. The potion had blackened the ends, but the color slowly returned to them.

Did it mean she was an undead?

Joshua's yelp broke her out of her circling thoughts. He was in trouble.

She raced down the two sets of stairs and on the far side saw Joshua prone on the floor. A dark shape leaned over his legs. She could see bands around Joshua's legs. There must have been a trap he had triggered.

The dark shape leaned closer and moved a hand to the back of Joshua's neck, and Joshua yelped in pain.

Rose swung at the monster, slashing through the arm that touched Joshua. The arm rolled away and dissipated in a cloud of smoke. The monster turned toward her. The head was all mouth filled with serrated teeth. It had no eyes and four arms that ended in tentacled fingers. She had no idea what it was, but it wasn't friendly.

It leapt at her, and she swung and dodged out of the way. The monster shrieked and fell away.

Rose rolled Joshua over. His face was gray, and his eyes were half closed. Black smoke surrounded his face, and he breathed it in with each inhale.

His eyes fluttered open. "Not...too...late, get...me...sunshine." He slumped.

Rose knew if she were alive, she wouldn't be able to carry him up the stairs and out into the sunshine as he wished.

But if she were undead, then she might be able to.

She lifted Joshua easily to her shoulder and carried him out into the sunshine. It only took a moment to lean him up against the stonewall of the tower. The sunlight pushed away the darkness that had gathered in his face.

His eyes snapped open, and he leaned over, coughing out more black smoke. His eyes were dilated and wide. She could hear his heart hammering as if he had run a marathon.

"It's okay. You're safe. We're outside." Rose sat next to him and rubbed his back.

He swallowed and nodded. "Y-you saved my life."

She had saved his life. She had saved a man who may hate that she was undead. Did it even matter how it had happened? With everything she'd lost, would her being undead make any difference? She still had no idea what was outside of the shield or how she would fit into it.

Joshua gazed at the woods. It was obvious he was thinking hard about something. "The HPA is looking for agents. Know anyone who might be interested?"

"I might." She needed to figure out what her next step was. She had nowhere to go and knew no one. Her mission was a bust. Her girls were already dead. She closed her eyes against the pain and pushed those thoughts away. What she needed was a purpose.

"What does the HPA stand for?"

"Human Protection Agency. We protect those humans who cannot protect themselves from the other creatures who would prey on them."

The idea that she could protect others was appealing. That would give her a purpose and aligned with her beliefs.

"I know someone who might be interested." She smiled at him.

Joshua searched her face and grinned back. "I can take you now."

2

ROSE

<u>Dawn, Primum second, 300 years post-Merge</u>

Five years later...

Rose leaned against the wall in her favorite shop and clenched her locket in her hand. The delicate gold chain dug into her fingers. The pain gave her something to think about besides her predicament. The Human Protection Agency was closed, because it had been infiltrated by a group wanting to UnMerge the worlds. Hopefully the HPA would open again soon. That was another story, but the lack of work left her at loose ends. She had too much time on her hands to think.

She needed a mission to distract her from the constant ache in her heart. Her girls were dead because she'd failed them.

The weight of that fact pressed on her chest, making it hard to breathe.

When she felt her worst was usually when her conditions surfaced. She waited for the chorus of voices to beg her to free them. She had no idea who they were, what they needed to be freed from, or if they were even real. Even worse, she had no idea when the eerie feeling of being watched by something malevolent would punch her in her gut. Something evil had been seeking her since she got to this city. She wasn't sure if the evil seeking her was related to the voices. Today, though, she felt nothing. Glenn's potion was still working.

"Were you interested in anything, Miss?" The dark-haired human smiled at her.

She snapped out of her circling thoughts and realized she'd been staring at a particularly ugly wrap. It was green, orange, gold, and purple, and not anything she would ever wear.

She smiled at the vendor, backing away from his stall. "No, thank you."

She stepped back into the crowd. She'd been wandering since morning, lost in her own thoughts, and hadn't realized how full the market had become.

Even the balconies of the apartments above the stalls overflowed with people.

Rose dodged a man calling out his wares on the edge of the street. Not only was the market packed with people, but they expanded into the narrower residential streets.

Music played and people danced. The day-loving creatures, like shifters, elves, and aeros, mixed and mingled at the market. Colorful fabric canopied the street, making everything look festive. The hawkers shouted their wares, and people packed together.

She was alone in the crowd. The only one not celebrating.

A pixie buzzed by, which drew her attention to the royal blue coat of the city guard standing at the corner. He looked at ease watching the throng. She gave in to her curiosity. It was rare for New Nadezhda's residents to be so jubilant.

"How long has this been going on?" Rose waved her hand toward the people.

"It's been like this since a few nights ago when the orange lines were in the sky."

She hadn't realized other people had known how close they all were to dying. She knew the orange lines were the seams of the world being pulled apart. The attempt to UnMerge the worlds had been thwarted by her boss at the HPA, Joshua, and his new girlfriend Serene. That also meant that this crowd was going nowhere fast.

To her right, a familiar cloak caught her attention. She'd seen that cloak every time she'd gone to Daniel's place. He must be out on official business, or he wouldn't be in his Master Phil disguise. People respected an older lone wolf who was a healer over a younger wolf. Her chest warmed. He had become her first friend who knew exactly what she was and didn't care. Their friendship, although only a week old, was cemented with the time they'd been quarantined together. She and Serene had brought an ailing Max to Daniel. He had recognized that Rose and Max were both contagious and prevented her from spreading it. Max had been unconscious and close to death. Daniel had almost died in the process.

He was fast, and it took her a moment to locate him in the shifting crowd. She caught up to him in front of a shop. The set of his body put her on edge. Something was wrong.

The shop looked like a typical herb, spice, and seed shop. Colorful canopies protected the wares on display from direct sunlight. On the shelves were wrapped bags of pre-measured dried herbs and spices, and seedlings in gift pots. The faint smell of loam hinted that the interior was probably enchanted to keep the products fresh.

The man sat behind the counter and looked as if he could reach the packets on the top shelf with his long skinny arms. The green tunic he wore meant he could also prescribe remedies for ailments. Nothing she saw explained the tightness in Daniel's shoulders.

"Are you sure you don't have any?" Daniel asked. His voice was mild and even, but Rose thought she detected an undertone of desperation.

"No." The vendor, looking snide, crossed his arms.

Rose came closer. She needed to use his disguise name. "Master Phil." She nodded her head in respect. "Anything I can help you with?"

Master Phil pointed at a packet on the third shelf behind the man. "I need some White Thorn."

Rose saw the white tag that clearly read White Thorn. "Is there a problem?"

The man made a face of distaste. "I don't sell to his kind."

"Well-known healers are a problem?" Rose asked, using her most innocent voice. She resisted the urge to punch the guy. Despite the fact that most of them thought little of packless shifters, Daniel had to be one of the best people she'd ever met. He'd dedicated his life to helping others. There were old-wives' tales that a shifter not in a pack was unstable. Add wolf and young male to the mix and folks thought he might explode at any time. If he were mated and had that bond, they would feel differently, but he was unattached.

"I would not normally come here. I am well aware of how he feels, but he's the only vendor on this side of the river who has White Thorn in stock." By his expression, Rose knew Daniel was very worried about a patient.

The man opened his mouth to give a retort when a scream erupted from the crowd.

A high-pitched, wailing female voice cried, "My baby! Undead have my baby!"

Adrenaline spiked in Rose's body.

Daniel lifted his nose to the air. "Over there."

Rose followed the sickly-sweet scent of decay around the corner. City Guards in blue had the crowd pushed back. One of them nodded at Rose, seeming to recognize she was from the HPA. The guards were smart to hold onlookers back. They would bring in a specialist to deal with the zombies. The undead were, at best, second-class citizens. At worst, they were hunted and killed.

A zombie bite or sometimes even a scratch and most creatures would be transformed into a zombie. The only reason people weren't completely freaked out was that zombies were dumb and generally easy to avoid. But they were always hungry.

The baby didn't have time for the specialists to arrive, so Rose had to intervene.

She followed the scent down the side street which dead-ended into a circle with a grassy area between houses. The zombie closest to the entrance turned and snarled. One pulled items out of a baby carriage, sending blankets flying. The third zombie grasped a baby barely old enough to hold its head up. The zombie's mouth opened, and he leaned toward the baby's head.

Horror chilled her. She jumped forward, drawing both her daggers.

Daniel charged the growling zombie in wolf form, opening up her path to the baby. Thank goddess he was such a fast shifter. She'd seen others take a full minute.

The zombie took the baby in its jaw.

She wasn't going to make it. "No! Put her back!" she bellowed as she leapt forward.

The zombie snorted and pulled the baby from his mouth. *"Sorry."*

Rose's momentum brought her close to the zombie. She took off his head and released the blade to snatch the baby. Then she turned and sliced his arm off, dropping the blade. Her instructor would've been irate with her, but it was the only way to catch the wailing baby. She pulled the baby to her chest as she rolled out of danger.

The sound of Daniel dispatching the other zombie eased some of her tension.

She turned the baby over, who was still sniffling, to see if she'd been hurt. The baby looked at her with big brown, red-rimmed eyes and wailed. Her little body stiffened, and her mouth opened wide.

Daniel, now in human form, slipped on his robe. Once he was dressed, he took the baby from her to examine. The baby stopped crying. "She's fine. Let's take her to her mom."

Rose let him take the lead, holding back. Had the zombie stopped at her command? Had it said sorry to her? She rubbed her head and hoped the voices wouldn't come back. Fear and unease tightened her stomach.

Rose knew which one was the mom because it took two guards to hold her back and her face was a frantic mess of tears. Her gaze snagged on Daniel holding her baby. "You saved her!"

The men let her go, and she snatched the baby from Daniel, hugging her close. "Thank-you-thank-you-thank-you." The rest was lost when she kissed the baby's head.

"No thanks are necessary, ma'am. Can you tell me where they came from?" Daniel asked.

The mom pointed to a smaller adjacent alley, which looked more like a shadow than an alley. Rose's heart dropped. There was probably a grate between houses. The system was archaic and only in some parts of town. Could a zombie make it up such a tunnel?

She walked down the buildings on each side of the alley, which almost brushed her shoulders as she walked. The alley smelled like garbage, but not like undead.

It ended after ten feet. There were no doors, just some

windows above that the residents used to empty chamber pots. The sewer cover was propped open with a stick, which left just enough space for a person to crawl through.

The crunch of a boot alerted her to Daniel behind her. She spun to confirm.

"Have you ever heard of zombies coming out of sewers?" Rose asked.

"No, never. They usually aren't coordinated enough." Daniel scanned the alley.

Rose leaned to look down the entrance. She couldn't smell the undead over the rest of the garbage and waste smell. "I don't think I can track them." It was unusual to have an undead in this part of town. Having three of them working together wasn't a good sign.

"We should shut the cover and report it," Daniel said.

Rose got the cover back on and stepped back in time to avoid being splashed by a chamber pot. "Let's get out of here."

The market crowd was still almost as thick as before the cry of zombies, if not for the extra City Guard blue, she'd have no idea anything had been wrong.

Daniel seemed to shake himself. "I still need to find that White Thorn."

"What's going on?" Whoever was sick must be in dire need.

"It's Max. He took a downward turn an hour ago. If I can't get the right ingredients to him by nightfall he'll die," Daniel said.

Rose's stomach plunged. Daniel had been able to stabilize Max, but hadn't found the key to helping him. The gunk that had been pumped into his body had been meant to turn Max into a Streg, one of the vicious undead that had been terrorizing the city. They were usually lost to blood lust and murder, but someone had been able to control them.

She had no idea if Max had been targeted, or if he had been a random victim. There was something about Max that seemed so familiar. She'd been drawn to find out more about him, as if he were an old friend she'd forgotten. It was one of the many reasons she helped Serene rescue him from the cemetery. It had only been a few days since they had liberated Max. "What can I do?"

"There's another vendor in West Market that sells White Thorn." He waved his hands at the press of people clogging the streets. "I can't afford to waste time getting through this crowd."

"You can shift into a wolf, you should have no..." She looked at the set of his shoulders and realized this other vendor must also not like packless shifters either. "I can get it. Meet you back?"

He nodded. "Thank you." His voice was gruff.

She squeezed his arm. "It's not a problem. I'll be right back."

His face softened. He gave her one of his shy smiles, then turned and was lost in the crowd.

The bridge she needed to cross was on the other side of the market. Perhaps she could go around on foot. But she couldn't waste time. Max's life was on the line.

The squat shack with the leaf roof next to her wouldn't make a good jumping off point, but catty-corner was a stone-worked building. Even though the bottom block reached to just above her head, the stones had conveniently large mortar lines. She would be able to use them to climb to the roof.

There were few beings who would be able to climb this stone wall. Her strength would help her. She went into the alley and ducked out of sight of the people on the street.

She made sure her weapons were secure and reached up to a grout line at about head level. She placed her feet flat and used them to stabilize herself as she pulled herself up. She reached to the next handhold and repeated her movements until she'd made it above the first solid block.

A few moments later, she stood on the roof, looking down.

The marketplace spread out below her. Throngs of people danced in the street. The zombie attack hadn't made a dent in the festivities. The celebrations extended past the edges of the market and as far as she could see. Amazement warmed her chest. People looked happy. Or maybe appreciative of being alive. The joy below her was in stark contrast with her own dark feelings. The worry for Max and her own restless guilt at having failed to save Hope smothered everything else.

She jumped to the next roof, landing lightly. If she jumped two roofs to the west, she should be able to see the bridge. Odds were good the river crossing would be full of people. There was no way that she was getting over the river quickly. The next nearest bridge was to the east. It would take her too long.

Two more jumps and the bridge came into view. It was as she remembered it, slightly away from the buildings. Under normal circumstances, there would be a grassy rise with a stone pathway leading to the overpass.

But today the hill was consumed by people. The scent in the air, even from here, was festive. Beyond their heads she could see the top of the wooden bridge. The distance across the river was just a bit too far to jump. She was strong, but not that strong.

The top of the bridge was made of two narrow arches of wood that connected to the wooden platform. The bridge itself was packed, but there was no one on the arches above.

She could use that as her route across the river. She could jump from building to building until she got close to avoid most of the people. If she jumped to an arch and then walked on the arch to the other side, that would be the quickest route.

The initial jump would be the hardest. Her martial art skill had been harder to keep in practice without a partner, but she did what she could. She'd added parkour to her training to make up the difference.

The arches had rope that went down as supports. She chose

a spot that was within her jumping range and had the best support, so she wouldn't affect the people on the overpass.

She leapt and landed lightly on one foot. Her Hapkido master would've been proud.

The wind tugged at her. A gasp from below had her glancing down. A little boy with bright red hair grinned at her. The tips of his ears and the faint scent of daffodils told her he was an elf. She grinned back and pivoted to walk up the arch.

The arch was six inches wide and curved up to the midpoint. Then it curved back down.

She walked easily to the top and across. It didn't take her long to find the vendor. He had the White Thorn and gladly sold it to her. She wondered how he would react if he knew it was for Daniel. She resisted the urge to teach him a lesson. She had to get back to Shifterville as quickly as she could.

She recrossed the river.

The feeling of being watched sent unease pooling in her belly. It wasn't the attention of the people below her, but something else. Something malevolent. Even in the bright sunshine and with the happy, relieved energy of the people around her, the feeling seeped around the edges of her mind.

It had stalked her on her missions. If she were to listen in that quiet place, she would hear its call.

She could hear it because she was a monster.

She did the only thing that had worked when it had gotten this loud before, before she'd had access to Glenn's potion. She ran across the arch and leapt to the nearest building and lost herself in the maze on the other side. She made her way closer to Shifterville.

Once at its border, she took an indirect path to Daniel's house.

Daniel opened the door at her knock. He'd taken off the disguise, but the gray powder still colored his hair to make him look older than he was. His face lightened into a big grin. "Rose. Do you have it?"

He seemed glad to see her. Heat flushed Rose's face, as she enjoyed that, for once, she was welcomed somewhere unconditionally. While Joshua had made her welcome in the HPA, no one else in the organization had done so.

"Is Max...?" Rose couldn't bring herself to ask if he was dead. She pulled out the packet of White Thorn and handed it to Daniel.

"Go sit with him while I get the potion ready."

"Sure." She walked into Daniel's front room.

A curtain cut off the view to the back corner where Max's bed was located.

Most shifters preferred to be home when they were sick. Since neither Rose nor Daniel had any idea where Max had come from and because of how sick he was, Daniel had decided to house Max in his own home. Again, that tug of pity and worry pulled at her chest.

She opened the curtain and walked into the space. Max lay on a bed against the wall. His skin was so pale it glowed next to the dark blanket tucked up to his shoulders. His dark hair stuck up in all directions in a spiky ball against the pillow. He looked strangely familiar, and yet she'd searched her memories and found no trace of him. Rose sat in the chair by the bed.

She examined him, trying to decide if he was still alive. He breathed, but she did as well, and she wasn't alive. He was cool to the touch, but different people had different temperatures. Had his hair grown? She held up his nails to see if they had gotten longer. Perhaps it was too subtle to see in a week.

Then, the real test. She took a deep breath to bring in his scent. He didn't smell like decay the way undead smelled. She didn't smell like decay, either, but she seemed to be the sole exception. But his scent wasn't quite right for a human. Perhaps he was a hybrid, a kind she hadn't met yet.

"Did you figure it out?" Daniel stepped around the curtain. He had a faintly glowing potion in his left hand.

"Figure what out?" She glanced at him but couldn't read anything in his blank face. "Is this one of those moments where you are trying to let someone figure something out on their own because it would be better for them?"

Daniel's face split into a grin and his eyes twinkled. He even gave a short chuckle. "Have him take a sip of this."

"What is it?" An odd protectiveness toward Max rose within her. She knew Daniel would never hurt him, but she still felt the hesitation. She'd been betrayed before. The odd thought made her swallow back acid. She didn't remember being betrayed, but knew she had been.

"It has White Thorn and some other ingredients. If my theory is correct, it will wake him up." Daniel held out the small glass vial.

"What do you think is wrong?"

"The art of healing is dependent on what species Max is. If I use the wrong ingredients on the wrong species, it can make them sick or not help heal them."

She let go of Max's hand and unstoppered the container. The aroma from the bottle was complex, but overall held a warm and spicy aroma. The smell was like nothing she'd ever scented before, but it made her mouth water. "What else is in it?"

Amusement flickered across his face. "Guess."

She watched his face and paused before taking a sip. He nodded encouragingly. She sipped and closed her eyes to focus on the taste. Warmth spread from her tongue to her gut, the way a good bourbon used to when she was alive. It left her feeling warm and full of energy. She shook her head. "I have no idea."

If Daniel said it would help Max, she'd believe him. She

gently put the rim of the glass to Max's mouth and tilted it so just a drop hovered near his lips. After a moment, Max's tongue darted out to the droplet. He took a deep breath. She brought the vial closer to give him more.

He swallowed the contents of the bottle and sighed.

A moment later, his eyes twitched open. Confusion marred the bright green of his eyes as his gaze trailed around the room. When his gaze met hers, his eyes widened.

"Rose?"

3

MAX

<u>Mid-morning, Primum second, 300 years post-Merge</u>

Max stared at the rising color on Rose's face as she jerked away. Her red ponytail and her face were the only things the same from the last time he had seen her. She was no longer in jeans and T-shirts but wore a leather shirt and pants. The shirt reminded him of armor, but like nothing he'd seen in Hope.

Confusion twisted his stomach.

"How do you feel?" The question brought Max's attention to a gray-haired man who stood near the side of the bed.

"Good." Max moved and felt surprisingly good, even if restless energy coursed through his body. Everything was clear and bright. He could see the freckles on Rose's cheeks. The faint smell of a dog was in the area. Perhaps the man had a pet.

Where am I?

The blanket on him was unfamiliar. This room looked nothing like rooms in Hope. The placement and the trim around the windows were wrong. A curtain blocked the view of the rest of the house, like they might find in a hospital room. Perhaps he was in the hospital. But even that felt incorrect.

"I am the healer, Master Phil. You've been in my care for over a week."

His accent was different than Max had expected. The word choice of healer seemed odd. "What happened?"

"What do you remember?" Something about the way he said it set Max's teeth on edge.

What *did* he remember? He'd crossed the shield. The crossing had felt odd, as if all of his body parts had stretched in different directions at the same time.

He'd woken up on his hands and knees with a view of a pair of dirty feet. Then sharp pain had radiated down from his head, leaving him in darkness.

Snapshots of a graveyard played through his mind and tightened his gut, but he couldn't land on any concrete images. It could've happened to him or could have been something he had read about. There were no emotions attached to the image. "Not much."

"Rose rescued you from the graveyard where someone was pumping you full of poison."

He turned his gaze back to Rose. She looked at him like she had no idea who he was. That was impossible. They had grown up in the same town, Hope. She had married his brother and been best friends with his wife. She'd been like another sister or a close friend to him. In fact, he remembered seeing her walk out of Mistress Yaneli's house days before leaving on his mission to save the town. He had asked how his nieces were doing.

The healer had said Max had been here for a week. But where was here? Unease raised the hairs on his neck. Maybe they had made it back into town. Which seemed unlikely.

"Are we back in Hope?"

Rose's eyes widened, and she took a step back. The sharp tang of fear filled the air. Her pulse beat wildly in her throat. She shook her head. "No." Her voice was a shaky croak.

"What do you remember?" Master Phil asked again.

"I crossed out of the shield that protects Hope, and don't remember much else."

"Hope?" Master Phil's gaze flickered to Rose before returning to Max's.

"The town Rose and I are from."

Master Phil's eyebrows hitched, and he glanced at Rose. His gaze stopped, and his expression softened. "Are you okay?" This was said much more gently than how Master Phil had talked to Max. Master Phil and Rose were friends. Perhaps lovers.

The idea twisted his guts. He stuffed the feeling away. Rose had been his brother's wife. His brother was dead now. She had every right to move on. Max just hadn't expected it to happen so quickly.

Rose jerked her gaze away from Max and looked at Master Phil, her eyes wide and round.

"You look terrified. What's going on?" Master Phil asked.

Rose shook her head. "I remember Max now. I don't want to talk about it." There was an undercurrent of sadness in her words.

What mattered was the mission. Now that he and Rose were together, they needed to complete their mission. The sooner they did so, the quicker he could go home. He desperately wanted to go home and see his wife, Eleanor.

Mistress Yaneli had said that she could only save his wife if he returned to Hope, having completed his mission. More unease tightened the muscles of his back. "We just got here, shouldn't we..."

"It's been five years!" Her shout and the anguish in her voice stopped his thoughts.

How could it be five years? He had just crossed over. But Rose's tone and expression supported that she thought they had long lost any means they could succeed on this mission. It couldn't have been five years. He would have some memories. She had to be wrong.

Max shook his head. "No, I just came over." He had to get back. His wife was waiting for him.

"Did you delay? Or did you come over a few days later?" Her voice was soft, but insisted on an answer.

"A few days." He cleared his throat. "Just like we were supposed to."

"Then you've been in New Nadezhda for five years," she said.

He gasped. The feeling of having failed made his body heavy. He still needed to go back. He needed to see the town for himself even if everyone might be dead already. He still had to go there and see with his own eyes what had happened to his wife.

"Let's pretend that I have no idea what you are both talking about. You explain, and I'll see if I can help," Master Phil said.

Rose's gaze shifted between Max and Master Phil's faces. She closed her eyes and sighed. "When the Merge happened three hundred years ago, a group of four wizards pooled forces and protected a human town. They put up a shield around the town of Hope. Something went wrong, leaving one wizard dead and two wizards trapped outside the shield. Only two stones remained from casting the spell." Rose and Max had both had a stone to cross over with.

Master Phil nodded. "That's the town of Hope that you're both from."

Rose flinched at the word Hope. She took another step toward the door.

"The people inside the shield have been having issues," Max said.

"What kind of issues?" Master Phil asked.

Max gazed at Rose until she answered.

"The crops failed, and sickness ravaged the population," Rose said.

"How do you two fit in?" Master Phil was watching Rose without seeming to, but Max could tell by the way Master Phil held himself.

"We were chosen to cross the barrier with the two stones they had. If we could bring together the four pieces of the stones that the wizards had used to put up the shield, then we could take it down." Rose paled and closed her mouth with a snap.

"How would that help?" Master Phil asked softly.

Max watched Rose, but she didn't seem to be able to form words. Her mouth opened and shut as if she were fighting herself. She paled even more, until her freckles looked black.

When the silence grew too long for him, Max said, "Mistress Yaneli said the shield had become warped and was making the people of Hope sick."

"Where were the stones supposed to be?"

"Mistress Yaneli said there would be an ally on this side of the shield who would help us." Max sat up and moved his feet to the floor. The floor was warm, which seemed weird. Floors in Hope hadn't been warm.

"It doesn't matter. I lost the stone. Our mission failed." Rose turned away.

The mission had never made any sense to Max. Why were their missions separated a few days apart? How could there be a contact on the outside if there was no way to cross the shield? But Mistress Yaneli had been confident, so he had done as she'd asked. Mostly because of his wife.

Max's heart clenched. When he had left, so many were sick —like his nieces, Rose's children. And they had already lost so many like his brother, Rose's husband. He and Rose were the only chance for Hope. They had to try.

Master Phil stepped forward, interrupting his thoughts. "May I?"

Max nodded.

Master Phil gently ran his hands down Max's neck, over his jaw, and raised his eyelid. "Open your mouth please."

Max did and Master Phil shined a light Max hadn't seen into his mouth.

"How is he?" Rose asked.

"Good. He's recovered well." And then softer to Max, "You may feel some fatigue in a few hours. This will work on Rose too." Master Phil handed Max a small bottle.

Max took the bottle and stood. That's when he glanced down and saw he was naked.

4

____

ROSE

Even though Rose didn't feel much like laughing, the expression on Max's face when he realized he was naked did make her giggle. It cut through the deep fear that choked her and gave her room to think. As soon as he said her name, a flood of memories flashed before her eyes and with them a tidal wave of fear and a wave of dizziness.

She hadn't felt this afraid since she'd first crossed over and found the necklace. Something was wrong with her. Maybe she needed to get her medicine from Glenn adjusted. That medicine seemed to be able to keep the voices at bay. Perhaps it could help control her fear.

Daniel seemed amused by Max's expression as well, but it didn't quite hide the concern in his eyes when he glanced her way.

She must really be losing it if Daniel left his Master Phil persona to express his concern. He was a professional healer, who tried not to pry unless the information would help him treat the patient. Or maybe they had just become that good of friends during their time trapped in his home. Rose and he had both thought he would die of the disease Max had been infected with.

Funny how almost dying tended to bond people, even an undead and a packless shifter healer.

"There's clothing out on the chair that should fit." Daniel parted the curtain and Max fled.

She shivered. Some part of her had known that Max was really his name. She didn't want to explore fear. She'd seen him strapped down on the slab with the green lines of poison flowing into his body, and had known his name was Max.

"Are you okay?" Daniel put his hand on her shoulder.

The warmth of his hand allowed her to calm down. Daniel was amazing. She took a long slow breath and forced her muscles to relax.

She nodded.

He seemed to search her face. "If—"

"These are too small," Max said from the other side of the curtain.

Daniel laughed softly and removed his hand from her shoulder. "I'll be right back." He left, and she could hear them talking quietly.

She knew the plague had killed not only her husband but her girls. Even thinking of the name of the town she was from made panic boil in her stomach and spread to the small of her back.

When Max and Daniel returned, she'd gotten herself under control.

"No way. There are shifters here?" Max's voice rose in surprise.

"Yes. The Merge brought many people together."

Max must have missed the droll undertone to Master Phil's voice.

"And vampires?"

Master Phil chuckled. "Yes."

"That is amazing." Max fidgeted with restless energy. He paused for a beat and caught Rose's gaze. "I want to get the stones to free Hope. There's still a chance they will help."

Fear rushed through her, starting at the front of her chest and expanding outward, until her fingertips tingled and her ears rang. She backed away and bumped into someone warm.

"What's wrong?" Daniel's voice was so close, the words ruffled the hair on the nape of her neck.

She shook her head, trying to put the overwhelming panic into words. Sounds distanced and she focused on breathing. She inhaled Daniel's wild aroma, a mix of wolf and sage, so close, and then on to Max's scent, which overpowered her with flashes of memories. She closed her eyes and mentally did her martial arts workout routine. The patterns calmed her.

When she could focus away from the scents, she realized Daniel held her in his strong embrace. She stepped out of his arms. He didn't resist her movement. She trembled and sat in a chair.

"This is not normal for her." Daniel stood next to Max. They both looked at her, making her feel exposed.

"The memories are overwhelming," Rose said. It was true, but not the whole truth. She was reluctant to mention the fear.

Daniel nodded, but didn't look convinced. "Maybe if we were able to unlock Max's memories we could find the stones and complete his mission."

"How do we do that?" Max asked.

"Rose said she found you in the cemetery. Someone was experimenting on you."

Max's jaw loosened. "So, you think that's why I can't remember anything?"

"Joshua Lighthouse recently broke a ring of people trying to UnMerge the world. The man who was experimenting on you was in that ring. Maybe Joshua has intel that could help you," Daniel continued.

The last tendrils of fear released her at the promise of the new quest. She grinned at Max. Even with the fear, having an old friend by her side again helped with the ache she carried with her.

Daniel opened the curtain. He wouldn't meet her gaze. There was something else. She stepped closer. "Daniel, what is it?"

The hardness behind his eyes softened. "I will go with you, my friend." He emphasized the word friend in an odd way that left her feeling confused.

"Are you okay?" Rose asked.

Daniel let out a small breath. His eyes were sad and lonely. "I had hoped. But it doesn't matter now." He shook himself. "Let's go find Joshua."

5

MAX

Max followed Rose out of Master Phil's house and onto a street like nothing he'd seen before. The lane was narrow with houses that leaned in. A misty cloud hovered around them as if the mist protected the lane. The furtive movement of claws on cobblestone raised the hairs on the back of his neck. The scent of wolves, foxes, and other creatures he had no idea how to classify swirled around him. Why were the scents so strong here? He knew without a doubt he was not in Hope.

He clenched his hand and felt no pain. Unease settled in the pit of his stomach. He'd cut the fleshy part of his thumb just before crossing over. The gash was deep enough he'd thought about getting it stitched. The urgency of his mission had made him just wrap it. When he'd gotten dressed at Master Phil's, he'd noticed there wasn't even a scar. Which meant it hadn't been just days since he'd left Hope. Perhaps Rose's statement of five years was accurate. The desperate need to see his Eleanor bubbled in his chest.

"How do we find this Joshua?" Max asked.

Master Phil grinned and threw back his head and howled. In the distance Max heard responses. They seemed to trail farther away and then come near again a few minutes later.

A howl sounded from a block away.

Master Phil cocked his head, listening, and howled back. "Joshua and Serene are near the West district."

"What is he doing over there?" Rose asked.

Master Phil shrugged. "Let's go ask him."

Max adjusted the satchel Master Phil had given him. He could hear the slosh of the potion he'd tucked inside a special pocket.

Master Phil darted ahead, leading back the way they'd come and then down a side alley, which was even smaller than the previous one. The alley ended at the side of a stone building. He could smell something wet and a slight breeze made him think the tunnel continued. Master Phil led them through the wall. As he crossed, the feel of magic tingled across Max's skin like cobwebs.

On the other side, the alley opened up into a broad lane. There weren't any people he could see, but he could still smell the musky scent of animals.

Instead of the same houses along the lane, the houses here were wildly different as if plunked down randomly. One house on the right was a two-story Victorian, like the one he lived in. The rest were squatter or narrower than the buildings he was used to. Some of the buildings were made out of something shiny or metallic. Others were whimsical, like the one across the way with trellises and flowers around a giant mushroom.

Rose took a deep breath. Her whole body tensed.

"What?" He smelled the air and when the breeze kicked up,

he caught the faint hint of rot. Unease raised the hairs on his neck. The scent was strangely familiar. "What's that smell?"

"Undead. Stay here." She took off running toward the smell. Master Phil followed close behind. They moved fast, and he was afraid that if he didn't follow them, he'd be left on his own in a city he had just woken up in.

She pulled ahead and was around the corner before he could catch her.

Damn it. He kept running, trying to locate the scent. When he rounded the next corner, the stench smacked him in the face and made him stagger back.

The faint sound of metal crashing into metal echoed up ahead. A weird mist pooled, making it hard to see exactly what was going on. He had no idea what undead were really like. Hope had some old books and DVDs with myths and stories, but that probably wasn't anything like reality. He grabbed a pipe from the ground just in case.

The mist shifted toward him and thinned. In an open space, which might once have been a playground, a dozen figures shambled forward. They looked like the zombies from the old movies. Their clothing was ragged, their motions were jerky, and they had odd bits of their bodies missing.

Rose jumped toward one, and his heart thundered. He hadn't seen Rose fight before. Her movements were confident and smooth as she avoided the zombie's grab.

"Save us." The words hung in the air. He wasn't sure which direction it had come from. He wasn't even sure if he really heard it.

Rose hesitated, and then her dagger slashed forward, and the head separated from the zombie. The body slowly collapsed to the ground.

Max jumped back, avoiding the still moving jaws. *Ugg.* Were zombie bites really as deadly as they were in old stories?

Rose moved on to the next creature.

A series of howls and yips came from the slide area. A pack of large, gray wolves took down zombie after zombie. One wolf would come from the front and dodge their clumsy attacks, then two would come from the sides and rip the zombie up. It was effective. He'd never imagined that wolves would be in a town fighting zombies.

"Help me." A voice behind Max made him turn.

Not two paces away, a zombie grunted. His clothing and flesh hung on his body. His white sightless gaze shifted to Max, freezing him. The zombie opened his mouth and grunted again.

Fear and horror chilled Max's blood and made it hard to move.

"Save us." The voice sounded masculine and nearby.

The undead shambled forward, past Max into the center of the block. There was movement in a bush. A wolf hid in the bushes. This wolf was smaller than those in the pack of wolves and didn't seem to be with them. The wolf watched Rose and didn't seem to notice the zombie lumbering closer.

When the zombie was within an arm's length of the wolf, Max shook off his trance. The wolves were helping Rose, so they must be allies. He needed to help this wolf.

Max ran forward and used the pipe like the baseball bat he'd used back in high school. The undead collapsed into a twitching pile.

The wolf sat up and tilted its head. The wolf's body rippled, his hair receded, and he stood up. The process didn't seem to be painful. There were no loud snaps or ripping sounds. His body just flowed and shifted until he was Master Phil again, who grinned at Max. "Thanks for the assist. There were too many of them, and I couldn't smell the zombie."

Wonder and amazement filled his chest. This world and its

people were incredible. Was the other pack of wolves also shifters?

"No problem. Who asked us to save them?" Max wondered if he had been hearing things. Where had that voice come from?

"I heard nothing. Are you okay?" Master Phil stepped closer, ready to help if he could.

Max shook his head. The voice must be a weird echo or his imagination.

Master Phil grabbed his clothing and put them on as he scanned the clearing. The man dressed fast. "Follow me," Master Phil said. He took off toward the far end of the clearing. The ground dipped and in the bowl, a mix of creatures Max had only seen pictures of in fairy-tale books and humans had corralled a half dozen zombies. Many creatures held long sticks they used to prod the undead, keeping them boxed in. The odd mist dissipated.

One cloaked man yelled out commands to the people around the zombies. Master Phil walked to the man.

"Max, this is Joshua Lighthouse." Master Phil gestured between them. "Joshua, meet Max, one of Rose's friends."

Joshua's eyebrows rose, and he nodded a greeting. Now that Max was this close, he saw that Joshua was heavily scarred on his face. His face wasn't pockmarked from a sickness, but looked like it had been scoured by scrapes and cuts.

"How did the zombies get to Shifterville?" Master Phil asked Joshua.

"I'm not sure. The city council has tasked me to go find out what's going on in the Necropolis. It's been locked down, so only one entrance is active," Joshua said. His gaze slid to Max, seeming to evaluate him.

A short, brown-haired woman who looked like Master Phil in the face stepped up next to Joshua. She reached up as he bent and brushed a kiss on his lips. "What did you need Joshua for?"

"Serene, this is Max, the man you helped rescue from the cemetery," Master Phil introduced them.

Serene's eyes widened. "You look much better. We all feared you would die."

Max wasn't sure what to think. Serene was related to Master Phil. They had an underlying similarity in smell and facial features.

"Trouble?" Joshua brushed his hand through Serene's hair in what seemed like an affectionate gesture.

"Nothing we couldn't handle." She grinned at Joshua who grinned back in response.

"Max has no memories of the last five years. Is there anything from what happened with..." Rose paused, as if choosing her words carefully, "the Streg that we could use to help him remember?"

Max had heard snippets of conversation and gathered that Streg were particularly vicious undead. He'd been rescued from someone infusing him with a magically enhanced troll disease to convert him into a Streg.

"The journal you found by Max in the mausoleum indicated Max was in the cemetery for a month or so, right?" Joshua asked.

Serene nodded. "There was nothing about where he'd come from, only about what had been done to him."

Max slumped. Without those missing memories from when he'd crossed the shield, he had no way of knowing where his stone had gone. If he had no stone, then there would be no way to see his wife and keep his promise.

"I knew it was a long shot," Rose muttered.

"Why don't you see if Wren can help? He's done some work in magically suppressed memories," Serene said.

"Most people can't just go in and see him," Rose said. "I'm not one of his favorite people."

Joshua chuckled. "Right now, I don't think I am either."

"Serene, would you mind taking him? You did say you wanted to visit Alesia," Rose said.

A strange look crossed Serene's face. She sighed and rubbed her eyes. "I would, but Alesia hasn't been back to the Rookery."

"Where is she?" Joshua asked as if he didn't really want to know the answer, but had to know.

"Guess." Serene stared at Joshua.

Joshua grimaced. "Ohhh. Wren is not going to be in a good mood. He probably won't help."

"We have to try," Max said. He didn't know Wren, but if there was the chance he could help, Max needed to attempt it.

"I'll go with Joshua to check out the cemetery. We could go back and see if there was anything we missed in the mausoleum where we found you," Rose said.

"That's a good idea. We did leave in a...hurry." Serene's eyes were full of humor.

Max nodded. It made sense to divide and conquer. "We can meet back at Master Phil's."

"I do have some appointments soon. I'll be at home," Master Phil said.

Max tried to smile at Serene, but the uneasiness was back. Serene had said 'magically suppressed memories.' Wren must be a wizard. Hopefully the wizards here were more open to helping others than they had been in Hope.

6

ROSE

<u>Noon, Primum second, 300 years post-Merge</u>

Rose walked next to Joshua as they headed toward the cemetery. The mist from the zombies still lingered lightly in the air, but faded with each step.

Remembering Max after all that time had been amazing, but also reminded her of Hope and the fear. A swell of conflicting emotions clogged her throat. Perhaps if she had a case she could dig into, she wouldn't have the tightness in her chest.

"So, what's going on?" Joshua asked quietly. His voice was soft and perhaps even kind. He had recently offered to be her friend no matter what.

It had been hard during the years she'd known him. She represented everything he'd hated. She wasn't human. She was hiding who she was. But still, strangely, he'd become her friend.

Perhaps he had sensed her loneliness. They had both been very careful to not share too much personal information. For her, it had been the fear that one wrong word would make him realize how different she was from what he thought. That worry still added an extra layer to the knot of turmoil. "Nothing."

He stopped at a corner. He peered around to check and make sure no one was following.

"I've never been introduced to any of your friends." He glanced back at her and seemed to do a swift assessment, which started at her feet and stopped at her hair. "You're upset."

She closed her eyes for a moment, suppressing a bitter laugh. She'd never been the recipient of Joshua's interrogation before. "Are you going to try to bribe or bully me?"

Joshua snorted, his eyes dancing with amusement. "Neither would work with you."

"Then what? Plant a double agent or get your information a different way?" Her voice sounded defensive even in her own ears.

"Perhaps." Then he reached out and touched her shoulder. A month ago, the move would've sent shivers to her stomach. "Or perhaps, my friend would want to share what is bothering her, so I can help."

The hot press of tears made her blink.

Joshua looked away. "You know you can trust me." It was an even statement that still had the power to pierce her to the bone. "You seem like you might need a friend."

There it was again. The overture of true friendship. His eyes and everything about the way he held himself said it was a true offer. To take his friendship, she would have to confess things she had never wanted him to know about her. She cleared her throat. She couldn't, not yet. "Let's go check out the cemetery."

Joshua nodded, but still looked troubled. "We can cross the river into the Southern Market."

Under other circumstances, they might have stopped at Joe's

along the way. The leader of the Hive always had information. "Stopping at Joe's?"

"Do you have anything you want to ask him?"

What could she ask? Did he know where Hope was? She didn't. Even thinking the name was enough to send chills down her back. "No."

"Maybe on the way back, when I have a lead on the case. So far I have no idea why the undead are still so restless."

"Could it be related to the Streg?" She and Joshua had been tracking down a serial killer in their city. It had turned out the killings were part of a plot to UnMerge the worlds. The last time she had seen him, before he broke the case, was when she had rescued him from a trap. Besides seeing the orange lines that had crisscrossed the sky, Rose had heard nothing but rumors about what had really happened that night. This was the first chance she had gotten to ask. "What happened?"

He glanced at her and then nodded. "I was born before the Merge. After the Merge, I was an orphan in the Archive. We found the Book of Secrets. It made me think my best friend was dead, when really he was plotting to UnMerge the worlds."

He paused, seeming to assess how she was taking his words.

Rose's belly fluttered in surprise. In the five years she had known him, he'd never said anything about himself. Her awareness of his history started when they'd met. The rumors about his past were varied, some claiming he was a demon spawn, and some claiming he had always been around to harass all the non-human species. He seemed to be waiting for her, so she nodded.

"Elder Martin and others murdered to get the ingredients to make a Streg army and cause the worlds to UnMerge," Joshua said.

Elder Martin had been a pillar in the community. The rumors about what had happened that night painted him as a victim of the tragedy. Why would Joshua or the HPA spread such rumors?

"The book was manipulating him. That's why the rumors were spread," he said as if reading her thoughts.

Rose shook her head. It was sometimes scary how in sync she and Joshua thought.

"There was a man who called himself the Creator, or Andre, who actually made the Streg. It was Andre's lair you and Serene rescued Max from."

Rose's gaze jumped to Joshua's face. What else had Serene told him about that night?

"It was the only thing she would tell me about that night. She said I needed to work through issues with my friends by myself." He leveled a look that said 'what can you do?'

Serene knew Rose was undead. That had been how they had escaped the undead who had boiled up around them when they investigated the graveyard just days ago. The fact that Serene hadn't told Joshua was good. While a part of her knew it would have been easier if Serene had told Joshua, it also wouldn't have been Rose's choice. Serene had gone out of her way to make sure she respected others' choices.

"Once Andre was dead, I thought the undead would go back to being dead." Joshua grinned ruefully and shrugged. "This is actually the third attack."

If Elder Martin had been creating a Streg army, what use would he have for zombies? Streg were intelligent, fast, and rage-filled killing machines. Zombies weren't smart and would head toward whatever was living with the sole intention of eating it. Trying to use a zombie army would be like sending a bunch of drunk HPA agents into battle. "Could someone associated with Elder Martin still be around?"

"Maybe. I'm supposed to meet an undead expert at the cemetery. His name is Calder." Joshua headed toward the bridge that spanned the central river. There was still one more intersection before they reached the actual bridge.

She kept her voice even. "Do you know anything about him?"

Joshua shook his head.

She knew that meant he wouldn't trust him. Joshua had been burned before. But she had earned his trust. And yet she couldn't trust him with her secrets.

What was the worst she thought would happen if she told him everything? He was living with Serene and seemed to have no issues now navigating between species. When she really looked at it, she was afraid he would no longer want to be her friend. She and Joshua had been through a lot together. The last case where he'd stopped the plot to UnMerge the world had changed him. Before that case, she never would have even considered telling him. But now...

They passed the road that led to Joe's and crossed the bridge across the river. The market was open on the other side.

"Serene would like that scarf." He glanced at the brightly colored fabric displayed in one of the stalls.

It did look like something her best friend would like. The thought made her pause. She hadn't realized that she considered Serene her best friend. Serene and her son, Daniel, knew more about Rose than anyone else in the city. Even Glenn, the man she got her tonics from, only knew so much.

"We can come back this way to get it for her."

"Do we need to look for a present for Max as well?" Joshua said it deadpan, but he happened to be looking her way when he said it. The sneak.

She stumbled, but caught herself on the wall. "Were you always like this?" she asked after an exasperated laugh. She realized she had no urge to get Max a present. He was still like a brother to her.

Joshua chuckled.

At the next booth was a leather bag with clips to add more bags. Daniel's bag was worn. This bag would make a great replacement. She'd have to come back and get it for him.

Once they left the market, they entered a neighborhood next to the west entrance of the cemetery. The ornate gate separating the neighborhoods was more about identity than protection.

Once they crossed the gate, the feel of the air changed. Something heavy settled on her skin, raising the fine hairs of her back and neck. Their foot falls echoed on the empty cobblestones.

At this time of day, she would have expected to see children playing in the streets or at least some shops open. But the doors and windows were closed and barred. The buildings felt abandoned.

There was something scrawled in black paint on the window of a door to her left. She took a step nearer. A strange symbol covered the glass. "Take a look at this."

It looked like a layered picture with a dagger on the bottom, then a stylized C, over a skull with flames flickering inside the sockets and a zipper across the skull's mouth.

"Recognize it?" he asked quietly. He took out a notebook and sketched the symbol.

"No." She stepped back, not wanting to be any closer to the symbol than she had to be. It made her skin feel too tight and added an ache in her belly.

As they walked, more and more of the symbols appeared on the glass windows and doors of the houses. On one house, every brick had the symbol painted in tiny lines. They were placed as if they were a talisman. She figured they were a protection against undead.

She turned the corner, catching the breeze from a different

direction. The stink of fear clogged the air. It wasn't sharp and new but lingered in the air.

She glanced at Joshua. His cloak was fastened in the front. The bulge there wasn't belly, but his bow. He'd strung it and hidden it under his cloak. For those who didn't know him, he would just look heavier. He probably had an arrow out and was ready to shoot.

She understood and itched to pull her daggers.

He must sense that something was off. "The neighborhood is afraid," he said softly.

"Undead escaping must not be a one-time occurrence." Rose followed Joshua around the next corner.

To the right, the cemetery fence stood out. Pale mist crept between the bars and spilled out on the pavement. There was still the impression of rocks and debris piled on the ground between the bars, but something wasn't quite the same as last time. She took a deep breath to see what she might be able to parse out of the scents in the slight breeze. Usually, when this close to the cemetery, she'd be gagging on the decay and rot, but she smelled nothing. Her unease grew.

That wasn't true. She could smell the man next to her and the faint aroma of Serene on him. She could smell the fear of the hundreds of people who lived near but weren't here. But no undead smell. Not even the smell of freshly turned ground. It was as if the cemetery were an illusion. The thought made her shiver in dread.

Movement at the top of a building caught her eye. A man stood on the roof on the corner nearest the cemetery. "They have guards." She flicked her eyes up to show Joshua where.

He paused on the cobbles and frowned. "Not a good sign."

"Should we talk to him?" She kept her voice light.

Joshua waved at the guy on the roof who climbed down the

side of the building. He approached confidently with his head high, but with a wary gaze.

"I was sent by the city's council to investigate the undead." Joshua pulled out the magical sigil that showed he was on a mission. "Is there anything you can tell us?"

The man's tight grip on his dagger eased. He cast a nervous look between Rose and Joshua.

"Last night was the third time a big group of them escaped, but we couldn't contain them." He rubbed his eyes, highlighting the dark shadows under them.

Her throat ached with sympathy with how hard it must have been to protect his neighbors. "Anyone hurt?" Rose asked.

The HPA training had sections on undead. She'd learned as much as she could to try to figure out what she was. Many people feared they would become undead if they were bitten or scratched by one. Only vampires and a few other intelligent undead could spawn. She didn't want someone innocent being spurned because someone thought they were undead.

"No, ma'am. We got lucky."

"Anything strike you as off?" Joshua asked.

She could tell by the way Joshua held his head and kept his face friendly that something about what the man had said struck him as odd.

"They don't come out in ones and twos, but in a group. We were easily able to take care of the small gang. But this last mob was far bigger."

Unease crept up her body. The unintelligent undead didn't seem to be aware of each other. They had escaped in ones and maybe twos periodically over the years. But never in groups. What other rules might be being broken?

"Are they only coming out at night?" Rose asked.

The man shook his head. "All the time. We're never safe." He closed his eyes and she noticed again how tired he seemed.

"How long has this been happening?" Rose asked.

"A week? Maybe more. It happened so gradually I'm not sure exactly when it started."

Joshua nodded. "How do they get out?"

"The front gates open. Doesn't matter what we have stacked against them or how securely we lock the door." The man sighed and rubbed his eyes again.

That was bad. Really bad. "Have you tried to magically lock the door?" Rose asked.

He nodded, his lips pressing in a firm line for a moment. She recognized the look. It was fear and frustration. "Nothing works."

"Has Calder been by?" Joshua asked it casually, but the way he was looking at the guard told her he was watching the man's reaction very closely.

The man gave a grim smile. "Yes, he helped put up charms to protect the families who live here." The man gestured to the windows. "He stopped the undead from breaking into the houses."

"Any idea where he's at?"

"He's usually by the west entrance. He should be there now. Just keep going that way." The guard pointed down the street the way they'd been going.

"Thank you." Joshua tipped his head to the guard, who shimmied up to higher ground.

"Let's check out the fence." Rose remembered the fence from her last foray into the cemetery. Serene being in the cemetery after dark had drawn all the mobile undead. Rose had had to get creative to rescue Serene and Max and get them over this barrier. She couldn't place why it seemed wrong now.

She led Joshua closer. The white mist swirled around the bars. As she stepped closer, she saw that the bars' metal was white.

"Did it look like that the last time?" Joshua asked.

"No." She reached out and touched the metal. Cold stabbed her fingers. She pulled her hand back with a hiss. She rubbed her fingers against her arms. She couldn't quite feel the tips of her fingers. "It's cold."

He reached out and touched the bars. "Very cold." He ran a fingernail over the metal. The white peeled away and dropped into his open palm. "It's frost."

The urge to tell him the truth overtook her. This could be how she started the conversation since they had different feelings about the fence. Her feelings might be because she was undead and could be a clue. "Did you feel anything else?"

He waited with the sliver of frost on the palm of his hand. It melted away. "No."

"There's something embedded in the metal to keep the undead away from it." She waited for him to ask how she knew.

"Is that new?" He frowned.

"Yes." She turned to walk away from the barricade. She could see him glance at her as they walked. He wanted to know how she knew, and he wanted her to trust him. She wanted to trust him as well, but the fear of being rejected held her back.

A few steps later, the gate came into view.

The gate towered above her. It should be a mix of cold iron and special wood, but the iron was white and the wood had just about splintered away. "Malani Necropolis" was scrawled across a plaque on one side of the gate.

"Are you here from the city council?" A deep voice boomed from behind her.

Rose flinched. She hadn't noticed anyone approaching. She turned to a wiry man with wild gray hair. His voice seemed far too big for his body. His eyes were a bright green.

"Yes, Joshua Lighthouse. At your service. You must be Calder." Joshua gave him a bow. "This is my colleague, Rose."

The man's eyes opened with what looked like surprise and

speculation. "I am Calder. I told the city council I had it under control."

"What can you tell us?" Joshua asked. He'd done this before. Distracted the person they were talking to so Rose could get a read on them.

She took her time to study the man. He was full human, but had the slight smell of decay consistent with him being an expert in the field of undead. It was hard to tell how old the human was, because of how unlined his face was. But something about his eyes made her think he might be far older than he looked. He wouldn't be the first person she'd met whose appearance didn't match their chronological age.

In humans, looking older than they were usually meant they'd suffered some tragedy, like the loss of a loved one. Suffering made their eyes look old beyond their years.

"It's only been a few days, but I think I finally have it under control," he said.

Was he lying or just naive? Sometimes the specialists she'd worked with in the HPA were very insular and had no idea how their area of expertise impacted others.

"Good. What was happening?" Joshua asked.

"The zombies were trying to form an infestation." The man sounded impatient.

The impatience grated on her with its sense of being out of place. He could be hiding his own lack of progress or something more sinister.

"Is an infestation a group of zombies?" Joshua asked.

"Yes and no. Under pressure, even the unintelligent undead can form a grouping that allows them to work as a team. A small group is an infestation. If a large enough group works together, you have a horde."

He must have seen the lack of comprehension on their faces. "Ever see a flock of birds and notice how they fly together and all turn at the same time? They somehow know what their neighbor is about to do?"

"Yes." She'd seen flocks of sparrows do that.

"Now imagine a thousand undead who are all going to the same place and all move together. All attack together. In the case of zombies, it's like they become a super organism of undead." Calder glanced at her.

Unease caused chills to race up her spine. If the undead were coordinated and controlled, they could be deadly.

"Do they become intelligent?" Joshua asked. She couldn't tell if Joshua believed the man. He kept his opinion hidden.

"They can if there are enough of them or if there is another intelligent undead that can act like the brain for the rest. Like adding a head to a body."

Rose shuddered at the thought. She was an intelligent undead, and she couldn't imagine being forced to connect with zombies. It would probably be like trying to use dead fish as arms. *Ugh.*

"That would be bad?" Joshua asked.

"Only if you have an issue with thousands of undead suddenly having a hive mind." Calder's voice conveyed his derision for their lack of understanding.

Something about the way he said it raised her hackles. There were vampires and other intelligent undead who might like to even the playing field with the living who kept their numbers low.

"Don't worry. Zombies don't like being near each other. They naturally resist forming an infestation, let alone a horde," Calder said.

The thought was comforting on some levels. The zombies would have to be forced to form a horde and wouldn't spontaneously turn into one.

"Then what happened here? We've had a number of reports of zombies attacking as a group," Joshua said.

Calder waved his hand as if negating the statement. "You may have had many zombies, but I can guarantee they were not cooperating."

Rose thought about that last zombie attack and had to agree. The zombies hadn't been coordinated. They had been like little kids playing next to each other.

"How can we tell if we get an infestation?" Joshua asked.

"They'll be a unit with one goal. They'll cooperate and act intelligently." Calder raised a finger with each point.

"A horde could be devastating to the city," Joshua said thoughtfully.

"What are the symbols you placed on the nearby houses?" Rose asked. The homes had seemed abandoned. The symbols made her feel uneasy, but she had no idea why. The guard had seemed grateful for them.

The man frowned at her. "The symbols are a protection. They keep the undead from seeing the life inside."

"We'd like to check out the cemetery," Joshua said.

Hopefully she and Joshua could find something to help Max and find the cause of the undead raids.

"I don't recommend it. It's dangerous for humans." Calder's voice was low and friendly. She wasn't worried, since she wasn't a human and knew Joshua could handle himself.

"We have to," Joshua said, matching Calder's tone. "Part of the job."

"I do have a few talismans I can give you that would offer some protection against undead. It will make it so the undead can't see you." Calder dug in his bag.

If undead couldn't see them, then Joshua wouldn't get mobbed by them.

Calder gave them each an amulet with a design similar to

the ones on the doors and windows of the nearby houses and buildings.

Rose took the amulet and put it around her neck. The undead wouldn't see her anyway. When she rescued Max, she had proven that.

Joshua put on his amulet.

And disappeared from her view.

7

———

MAX

<u>Afternoon, Primum second, 300 years post-Merge</u>

Max stared up at the huge tower. It looked like the pictures of skyscrapers from before the Merge, except the top had many large balconies. "This is the Roost?"

Serene nodded and pushed her hair out of her face.

They had walked across town in silence. He hadn't been able to concentrate on the cool speculative glances she gave him with all the wonders around him. Everything seemed even more magical than living in Hope, where most of the residents were wizards. It was the colors and juxtaposition of so many different elements. The familiar mixed with the fantastical with almost every stride. A pixie fluttered past. There was an actual toadstool with what had to be a gnome sitting on it.

"I still can't get over seeing fairy folk and other people from the books I grew up reading as folklore." He knew he must be grinning from her answering smile.

The set of Serene's shoulders relaxed. "I wasn't sure how you'd take it."

"What?"

"Seeing your nightmares for the first time." She said it blandly, but seemed to watch him from the corner of her eye.

She acted as if she had been hurt before and perhaps even misunderstood. He'd dealt with being misunderstood by being one of just a handful of non-magical humans in Hope.

"Some of the stories don't paint the people from myths in the greatest light. I think the biggest clashes were when human culture and expectations met a different set of norms."

"We still have that issue," Serene said. "It helps to have an open mind." She seemed to be thinking about something in the past. A small, bittersweet smile crossed her face.

He didn't want to ask about the smile. He was sure that was a story unto itself. But he did wonder about the previous conversation. Was there a chance Wren wouldn't help him?

She led him down a road that ended at a large golden gate. Blossoming vines entwined the bars, which made the gaps between them small. Two guards stood just inside, watching them. He couldn't see them clearly, but they looked human.

"Do you think Wren will help me?" Max asked. For a reason he couldn't pinpoint, he trusted Serene.

"He might. He blames me for his sister leaving."

Max winced and then nodded. He could understand being protective of a sibling. He'd felt the same way about his family. When his wife had been sick, he hadn't been reasonable. He hadn't wanted to leave her side. What would he have done if she had been gone? He shivered. Wren might not help them.

Serene straightened her shoulders and stepped to the gate. The guard glanced at Serene who grinned at him. "Hi, Ian. I came to see Wren."

The gate opened enough to let the guard step out. Max's

heart stopped. The man looked like an angel with the puffy, white wings that lay near his back and with his golden, shiny armor. The only difference was that instead of hair, a crest of feathers started at his forehead and traveled to his back.

"Is that wise?" The man looked serious and a little nervous.

"He's not doing well?" Serene asked softly, crossing closer to the guard. Her face and body language clearly said she cared.

"No." A flash of worry worked across Ian's face.

"Maybe I can distract him?" Serene's voice was coaxing.

"It's your wings." The guard shrugged and then turned his pointed gaze to Max. Even though he acted like he didn't care, the set of the shoulders said he was relieved someone was here to help.

"I'll take that chance." Serene nodded. "This is my friend, Max."

The guard cocked his head and scanned Max.

Max wasn't sure what the guard was looking for, but there was the slight tingle of magic in the air. He felt like he was on trial, but had no idea why. He took a breath to calm his nerves and nodded. Not sure what customary greeting would make the guard feel better, but knowing if this option failed, he worried there'd be no more options for finding his memories.

The guard gave a sharp nod, and the gate behind him opened. "He's in his office."

Max followed Serene into the entryway.

A luxurious garden was nestled around the tower. Large, white flowers and a sweet scent he didn't recognize filled the air. Ivy clung to the wall and draped over an entrance to the tower.

Serene closed her eyes in the garden for a moment and then waved him into the tower entrance.

He stopped after taking a step inside. He'd been expecting something drab and functional, but instead the walls were crystalline and white. The whole room felt open. A set of marble stairs hugged the wall to his right.

"It's going to take a while to walk up the stairs. So, we'll have to talk." Serene couldn't quite hide her curiosity about him.

He looked up the spiral, and it seemed to go on forever. "How many stairs are there?"

"We have to go to the top." She grinned. "So, there's plenty of time to get to know each other."

"Won't we be overheard here?" he asked softly. This didn't seem like the best place to have a conversation. He wished he would have talked while they walked here.

"The Aeros take privacy very seriously. They will not intentionally listen."

"What about whoever else lives here?"

"Anyone here is a friend of the Aeros and respects their wishes."

Could he trust her faith in the Aeros? "Why do you trust them?"

Serene gave a sad smile. "When I lost everything, they took me in. It was a great risk to their whole colony. I'm sure that without their help I'd be dead now." Her eyes were clear and sincere. Nothing he had to say was a secret. If he freed the people of Hope, then many, many more people would know about them.

He started up the stairs, taking them at the same pace as Serene. "What did you want to know?"

"How do you and Rose know each other?"

He gave a thought to how much to tell her, but finally decided that if both Rose and Master Phil trusted this woman and his own instinct was to trust her, then he was better off telling her everything.

So he told her about the wizards and the town of Hope. He

told her about the troubles and the famine and sickness. He even told her about his little sister who had been one of the first to die of the plague.

"Were you and Rose friends?"

"Yes. Just about best friends. We went to school together, and we were in the same circles."

"What circles were you in?"

"I had no aptitude for magic, unlike most kids in the town. I mostly liked to read. My little brother was the man Rose eventually married."

"Rose is married?" Serene's voice squeaked.

"He died after my sister did." The ache in his chest was still there from losing his siblings. He remembered Rose at the funeral. Her face had been composed, but her eyes had been wild and hurt. Her two daughters had clung to her hands. Eleanor, his wife and Rose's best friend, had been torn over who had needed her more. Finally, she'd decided to bring them together for a group hug.

The clear sunlight warmed him through the windows.

"If it hadn't been for Rose's two girls, I'm not sure what she would have done."

Serene stopped on the stairs and stared at Max. "Rose has children? Tell me they didn't die as well." She rested her hand on his arm. Her eyes were wide, watching him, as if willing him to say they were alive.

When Mistress Yaneli had asked him to go on this mission, he'd been reluctant. Once he discovered the mission was linked to saving his wife, he readily agreed. Why he'd done it made sense, but why Rose had gone made no sense. The image of her arms around the girls came to him. Grief swamped him. Not only for himself at losing his siblings, but at the pain Rose had suffered.

"No, they were alive when we left. I was shocked that Rose

was willing to leave. Those girls meant everything to her. Especially after my brother passed." He hoped his nieces were alive and well and safe with his wife. His wife and the girls were his only surviving family.

He went on to tell her about Mistress Yaneli and the plan for Hope. "So that's why I'm here."

"Rose has been here for at least five years," Serene said.

Max shut his eyes and paused on the stairs. The thought made him very uneasy. What had happened to him in those years? Part of him hoped they were wrong somehow. "Are you sure?"

Serene nodded and urged him to keep walking. "Rose's reputation is almost as formidable as Joshua's. They have been a team for over five years."

That left him with gaping holes in his memories. Hopefully, Wren would have some idea how to restore them. Max still only got flashes of graves and the feeling of being trapped when he thought about the immediate past.

"The last thing I remember is leaving Hope through a shield that looked like a large bubble. It had that same rainbow sheen." He could still taste the strange potion Mistress Yaneli had given him to cross over and the press of the package with Mistress Yaneli's own stone from the original spell.

She had wrapped her hand around what had looked like an ordinary gold necklace with a small cross and pulled it from her neck. When the chain snapped, the necklace transformed into a stone with a fire symbol strung on twine that rested in her hand.

He'd stepped through the shimmering field and experienced the sensation of some unseen force pulling on his arms, legs, and head as if he were a piece of taffy being stretched. When he opened his eyes again, he'd been on the ground at eye level with a pair of dirty feet.

Max stubbed his toe on the stair, which pulled him from his

thoughts. He told Serene about the dirty feet and the vague memory of many gravestones.

"So, you could have been here that whole time. I wonder where you were?"

"What do you mean?"

"You just seemed so surprised by everything. It's like you were never actually in the city proper."

He thought about his wonder as they'd crossed the city. Everything had seemed new and magical.

"Where would I have been?" Since his only memory was of gravestones, maybe he'd been in the cemetery the whole time. Serene and Rose had found him in a cemetery.

Serene shook her head. "We only have a few more floors and we'll be at the top."

It occurred to him that while he had missing memories, Rose had five years' worth of experiences he didn't know about. It was odd to think his knowledge of her could be so out-of-date.

"What can you tell me about Rose?"

"She and Joshua have been good friends. She's about the only person he trusts. They've been through a lot together."

Good friends could mean she and Joshua had been lovers. The thought of Rose with another still made him uncomfortable. He wanted what was best for Rose and had worried she might never love another after his brother had died. He knew five years had passed since his brother had died, but it didn't feel like five years.

"Were they...?"

"No. I don't think their relationship ever went that way, but with her background, I can see why Joshua would be her friend. He was always drawn to help others." Her expression was wry but affectionate at the same time. "Here we are."

Max looked up and saw a massive pair of doors. They looked to be made of thick, solid wood. The hinges were oversized, and the locks were also large. Intricate patterns covering the entryway looked like nothing more than flowers and vines, but a slight tingle in his skin told him there was magic. Was this big, heavy, bespelled door for keeping people out or in?

"Hi, Eliot and Perseus. We are here to see Wren."

Max hadn't noticed the two guards on either side. They were dressed the same as the other guards but seemed even more massive. Perhaps the magic had hidden the guards from his sight.

"Is he expecting you?" one of the guards asked.

"No," Serene said.

The guards didn't move. Even though they were still, Max could sense their uneasiness. All was not right behind that entrance. They weren't going to let them in. He also knew unless they were allowed in, Max had no way to get past the guards, let alone the door.

"Please let me in. Maybe seeing me will get him out of his funk," Serene said.

The guards' eyes widened, and they exchanged a look. One of them flushed, and the other seemed uncertain.

"I swear to not tell anyone what I see inside," she said solemnly, raising her hand to her heart. Did people here cross their hearts like they did in Hope? Was what was behind the door possibly so horrific it required promises to keep it under wraps?

"I swear as well," Max said. He moved his hand to mimic what Serene had done.

The two guards exchanged another look, and then the one on the left said, "Go in, but be careful." The guards opened the doors.

Relief warmed him. One more obstacle out of the way. Hopefully, Wren would be willing to restore his memories.

Serene stepped in, and he followed her into the biggest

library he'd ever seen. Shelves filled with books went from floor to ceiling along the walls and in the middle of the room. Even though this seemed like a library, it was too quiet and still. He had a bad feeling about being here.

The door clicked shut as soon as he passed the threshold.

Serene sniffed the air. "Do you smell that?"

Max sniffed as well. He picked up the scent of wet bird and something that smelled of honey and fermentation. "Yes. What is it?"

Serene sighed, looking sad. "It means things are worse than I thought. Let me do the talking."

They moved into a room full of books. His fingers twitched with the desire to snatch one off the shelf and see what was inside. Even the library at Hope hadn't seemed to have the sheer number of tomes he saw lining these shelves. The variety of books was staggering. Some were small and some were large. Some were ornate and some were plain. Different languages caught his eye. Were the fine stylized letters elven? He had no idea. The whole room seemed even bigger now that he was walking amongst the rows.

"You like books." It was a statement. She guided them between the bookshelves toward the far side of the room.

"Each one holds a promise of something new. A distillation of a story or of knowledge." He whispered what his teachers used to say. They rounded a corner where the smell was strongest and came to a dead end. The floor was empty.

What the heck? He'd been expecting someone sitting in a chair reading a tome, or at worst, sprawled on the floor.

"Where is he?" She looked puzzled. She paced forward and touched the end shelf.

Max glanced around and then up. Just above their heads, another Aero peered down at them. His bloodshot eyes watched them with disinterest. Max sucked in a breath and stepped back. He should have known that someone with wings would pick somewhere high to rest.

Serene followed his gaze. "Blazes. He's drunk."

8

ROSE

<u>Afternoon, Primum second, 300 years post-Merge</u>

Panic crushed Rose. She reached forward and grabbed where Joshua's arm had been before he'd disappeared. She had to tell him what was going on without letting Calder know. The amulet that stopped the undead from seeing them was now stopping her from seeing Joshua.

Anyone who saw she couldn't see Joshua and knew what the amulet did would know she was undead. At best, the undead were second-class citizens; at worst, they were hunted and killed. She shivered.

"Are you okay?" Joshua's disembodied voice asked. He sounded worried.

"Yes, let me go first." She shot a glance at Calder who had his eyes narrowed at her in what seemed like speculation. Fear tightened her throat. He was an undead expert, so she didn't want him to get interested in her. She needed to act natural and get out of his sight.

She released Joshua and walked to the gate. *Just act normal.* She lifted her chin, trying to appear confident. Once she and Joshua got into the cemetery Calder wouldn't be able to watch. She opened the gate and stepped in.

The cemetery seemed quieter. Was that just fear muting her senses? She scanned the area, alert for any movement. A few squirrels hopped in the branches, but everything else was still. She could still feel Calder's interest. A few moments later the gate closed.

She took a deep breath. She was going to have to tell Joshua about being undead. He already must know that something was wrong.

She turned back to the gate. Joshua still wasn't visible, but she could still see Calder on the other side of the gate, so she lowered her voice. "Joshua, I can't see you."

He said nothing, and she strained her eyes to see him. His scent was nearby, but she couldn't orient on it. The muscles in her shoulder tightened. Was Joshua still even there? Was she alone in the cemetery? She knew he wouldn't abandon her. Not yet anyway.

Something closed over her shoulder and she stifled a scream. She reached up and found an arm that smelled like Joshua.

"Why can't you see me?" Joshua sounded puzzled, not angry.

A slight bit of relief warmed her. She wasn't sure what to say so she went with simple. "The amulet makes it so I can't see you."

She suddenly felt breathless. This was the core of what would drive Joshua away. If this had been a month ago, she knew he wouldn't have forgiven her for lying to him all these years. If it wasn't for Calder, Joshua never would've needed to know what she was. She wouldn't have been able to survive if this had happened before Joshua had met Serene. She wasn't exactly sure what he would have done, but driving her out of the HPA was high on her list of guesses. He'd been very intolerant of Others.

"Because you're undead?" Joshua asked softly. She couldn't see his face to tell what his tone meant. Did he hate her?

She could feel heat flush her face. The rush of embarrassment and regret and worry tangled her up. She opened her mouth to say it, but the words stuck in her throat. She swallowed and nodded instead.

As the silence continued, she imagined how he was taking it. He would hate her. She would lose the oldest friend she had. Serene already knew, but maybe he would prevent them from being friends. What would Daniel think when he found out? Anguish clogged her throat. She'd be alone again. Any friends from Hope were already lost to her.

When the HPA was reopened, she wouldn't be invited back. In fact, Joshua could go to Joe and spread the word that she was—

"Whatever you are thinking, stop it." His voice sounded exasperated. Not angry or judgmental. "You're still my friend. We need to talk through our relationship and mistakes I've made. But we have to wait for a safer time."

The swell of emotion in her chest surprised her. It was warm and light and made her feel a little shaky.

Joshua appeared in front of her, looking concerned. He had the amulet that prevented him from seeing her in his hand. It must only work when it was around a person's neck. He stepped forward and pulled her into an embrace like she was a little kid who needed a hug. She did need a hug, so she hugged him back.

Relief and worry snarled in her chest making it hard to breathe.

"You okay?" He stepped back so he could see her face. His expression was concerned.

She swallowed again and nodded.

"Liar."

She almost laughed and felt another surge of relief. He really did care.

A grunt ahead drew her gaze to the bushes nearby. A skeleton looked up at them. Its dry, cracked bones creaked as it moved. Disgust soured her stomach. This was what she was. Undead. "Put your amulet on before we blow this mission."

He stepped back and as the amulet settled on his chest, he disappeared.

The skeleton walked closer and then right past them without stopping. At least if she had to be an undead, she preferred to be an intelligent one.

"What are we looking for?" he asked.

She gave a shaky laugh. "I have no idea."

"There's nothing wrong with using what you were given to solve a problem. You were here before whatever happened. What's different?"

She took a breath and closed her eyes. "The iron in the fence was different. It stung me." The last time she'd been able to hop the fence with no issue. She'd found a pole to help Serene over. The image of Serene clinging to the top of the pole made her smile.

"What else?" Joshua urged.

"There's less of that protective wood on the gate."

She took a breath, opened her eyes, and scanned the area. There was still a mist above them and some creeping between trees. The area where they stood was open to the sky, with low, gray grass and paths that led between gravestones and trees.

She glanced back the way they'd come. Joshua was right, the whole feeling here was different. Before, even though she had known they wouldn't attack her, she had been prepared for an attack because of how many undead there were. She didn't feel that way now. This time she'd been willing to have a personal conversation with Joshua. That never would have happened last time.

"This gate was unlocked. The other one was wedged shut."

She took a deep breath, drawing in the local scent as she had done outside of the fence. Unease hit her again. She should be able to smell the rotting now. There should be nothing blocking their scent.

"The smell. I can't smell the undead any longer. Like something is blocking them or my senses." She dared to open her eyes. Joshua was still gone, but she could still smell him in the area. "There aren't as many wandering skeletons or zombies. Serene was attacked within moments of walking into the cemetery." It was too quiet. Where were the undead?

"Maybe the zombies and skeletons are being kept somewhere." His voice came out of the emptiness, but she could imagine Joshua's eyes being unfocused in thought.

Zombies and skeletons were dumb. What intelligence they had when they were alive was long gone. Why would someone want to take them from the cemetery?

"Why?"

"What if someone were trying to create a horde?"

The unease pooled in her belly and twisted.

"So, you think locking up the zombies together might make them...bond?" The idea of someone building a horde was horrifying. Not the undead themselves, but having coordinated zombies as an army. The city would have a hard time dealing with their own dead coming back to take over.

If she were in charge and trying to take over, she'd send the horde to the areas they had lived in when they'd been alive. Such an army would have an advantage because the remaining family might hesitate to kill Grandpa, but Grandpa wouldn't hesitate to kill them. She shuddered at the thought.

"Someone keeping the zombies and skeletons somewhere

else would account for why you can't smell many of them. The mist is thicker around the edges. Did it feel funny?"

"I didn't really want to walk through it." She thought about her aversion to the gate. Could it have been a combination of the fence and the mist causing the feeling? The mist the last time had felt different. She hadn't noticed any aversion to the mist, but had been strangely comforted by it.

"The infestation of undead from Shifterville had that mist around them," Joshua said.

She thought back to the attack. "I don't think they were really bonded. They didn't act like they were of one mind." She walked slowly forward down one of the trails. The zombies in the market had done as she'd asked. It was against what they would have done. Was that the start of a bond?

"Failed experiment?"

Max had been experimented on here. Maybe there was a connection. "We found Max in a big mausoleum."

"I know where that is. Let's go check it out." His boots crunched ahead.

"You know I still can't see you," Rose said, slightly exasperated. Joshua was acting like he had already forgotten she was undead.

"Did you want me to hold your hand?"

"Serene would kill me," she said, half joking.

"You're the little sister I never had. She'll be fine."

Rose expected that categorization to hurt. She'd always known that her crush on Joshua would go nowhere. Not only was he alive and she was undead, but they weren't suited. But his statement didn't hurt, it felt right.

Joshua took her hand and led her down the twisty paths. Even holding his hand, she didn't feel half the pull she did toward Daniel. Which was unsettling.

Joshua never hesitated when they came to a crossing.

This time through the cemetery with Joshua was so much different than her last time with Serene. There were no stirring undead. The graves to the right looked empty. Maybe Joshua didn't even need the amulet. It would be easier to move without it, but if there were hidden undead, they would be drawn to Joshua's life force. It would cause a fight and if there was someone in the cemetery, it would alert them. "Could you take off the amulet for a moment?"

He released her hand and was suddenly visible next to her. "What's up?"

"Stand here for a second."

He did. She listened and heard nothing. She remembered how the undead had been drawn to Serene. Rose had an odd feeling. It was the type of feeling she had learned to listen to. But she didn't quite understand what it was trying to tell her.

"Take off your amulet," Joshua said.

She took the necklace off. The feel of the air around her changed. She felt hemmed in. Trapped. She could feel the press of too many undead nearby.

It wasn't a scent, but a strange feeling in the pit of her stomach. She'd known where the undead had been the last time she was here. She looked at the amulet. It looked relatively simple to craft. The feeling that something was very wrong and they were overmatched grabbed her by the chest.

"I think we need to come back later, without the amulets," Rose said.

Joshua raised his eyebrows, but nodded. "I trust your judgment. What does it feel like?"

"Like a thousand people crushed together. They're half awake and waiting." She glanced at him to see how he took her words. She felt vulnerable talking to him so openly. Was there something she would say that would break their friendship?

He shivered and nodded. "The center of the cemetery has

something hungry. It's moving, but waiting for..." He half closed his eyes as if he were using a different sense.

"How do you know?" She thought about the strange hunches and knowledge he'd had all the years she'd known him. It felt as if he were letting her see the real him as well.

He glanced at her and his face reddened. "I have a power I got when I lived through the Merge. I can detach a part of my soul and send it on missions."

The confession shocked her. He had always seemed so normal. So human. He had a formidable reputation as a human protector and had not always been kind to other species. Yet she had never told him about her being undead, so why would he tell her about his powers?

"I was afraid to. And in denial." He shifted his gaze to her face. He had on his poker face, with his emotions blanked from his expression. "Still buddies?"

The stillness after he asked was a tell. He was waiting for her to reject him. She almost laughed. "Still friends?" she asked him back. Relief pushed hard against her ribs. Maybe she had been worried for no reason. Perhaps they each had had secrets and were willing to now truly be friends.

He grinned. "Yeah. Let's get to the mausoleum."

A few moments later the lone building appeared in the mist. Rose still didn't sense anything but solitary skeletons. The door was ajar. The darkness seethed like a living thing. She paused to use all of her senses. "There was a torch to the left."

A pale blue glow shot forward, pushing back the darkness to reveal the short hall. "I got it," Joshua said.

Rose followed the light into the room. The slab of white stone was still there, but there was no green ichor or indication that Max had been tied to the slab.

The table against the back wall where Serene had found the journal was gone.

Everything was swept out and clean. The hairs at the back of her neck stood.

"I take it the room didn't look like this the last time you were here." Joshua walked to the far corner and paced back.

Rose shook her head. "That means we missed someone from the UnMerge attempt."

Joshua looked as uneasy as she felt. He ran his finger along a ledge and it came up clean. "Let's head back. We won't be finding any clues here."

9

———

MAX

Max pulled Serene behind him as the bottle fell out of Wren's hand and crashed to the floor, shattering. The glass sparkled between the bookshelves and the fermentation and honey smell surrounded him.

"What are you doing here?" Wren's voice was slurred and sounded only mildly interested. He looked down from the top of the shelf.

"We need your help," Serene said.

"Why would *I* help *you*?" He may have been trying to be scornful, but his tone hit sad instead. He rubbed his eyes, looking devastated.

"Then help Max," Serene said.

"No." Wren turned away.

Max's stomach dropped. Wren was his best hope of getting his lost memories back.

Serene grabbed Max's arm and mouthed, "Talk to him."

Max gaped. What was he supposed to say to Wren to make him help him?

She rolled her eyes at him as if she thought he were being dumb. What did she think he could say? What did he even know about Wren? Only that he was a mage and knew everyone in the magical community and that he blamed Serene for his sister leaving. Maybe that was where to start.

"I lost both my sister and brother."

Wren didn't move and for some reason it annoyed Max. Wren hadn't lost his sister forever, they just weren't talking to each other right then. It was much easier to fix not talking to her than to fix her being dead. "Your sister is alive."

Wren flinched. Whether at Max's volume or his words, Max wasn't sure.

"Mine isn't. I would give *anything* to have my little sister back," Max said.

Wren turned and stared at Max with wide eyes. Max felt a sinking sensation that perhaps he had gone too far, but something needed to get Wren to put his issue in perspective. Max decided to really push.

"There was nothing I could do to save her, and she died in my arms." Max's voice rose and shook at the end. "Alesia is still alive. Do you know what that means?"

Wren shook his head.

"It means you still have a chance to make it right." Max stared into Wren's eyes.

Wren was the first to look away. He still didn't look convinced. But Wren's quick glance at Serene made Max think that Wren needed a moment of privacy to get through his emotions.

Serene backed up a step, her eyes almost as wide as Wren's. She looked between the two men as if she'd expected Max to do something else. He had no idea what she wanted him to do. They really should have talked on the way here.

"He needs a bath and some food. Maybe some tea or something. Can you help get him something to eat and drink?" Max asked.

Serene nodded. "I'll have the servants draw him a bath and get food."

"Take your time," Max said.

Serene hesitated but walked away. When the room's door clicked and he was pretty sure she was out of the room, he turned back to Wren.

Wren looked to be deep in thought. Perhaps Max's words had shocked him out of his funk. Maybe it was time to extend an olive branch.

"Did you want me to help you down?" Max asked.

Wren jerked, and then a haughty, snotty look filled his face. "As if you, weak human, could."

Max took a breath. Anger flowed through his veins, heating his skin. He needed Wren to take him seriously. He needed Wren to understand that Wren could fix his relationship with his sister.

Once he realized that, then Max could ask him to fix his memories. There must be a clue that would help him succeed in his mission and see his Eleanor. A sharp longing filled his chest, making it ache. It added to the mix of emotions rioting within him.

Max climbed the shelves easily. As Max reached the top, Wren rolled onto his back and crossed his arms. Inch-thick straps ran across his chest and over his shoulders, forming what looked like a harness. They seemed sturdy and would provide a place to hold on.

Max grabbed the straps and tugged. Wren's body moved. Good, they should hold him. Max tightened his grip and pulled

Wren toward the edge. When Wren was at the edge of the shelf and Max was almost off balance, he jumped away from the shelf. The stone groaned as Max landed. He carried Wren over to a chair and dumped him on it.

Wren gaped at Max and clutched the straps. *Good, he's paying attention.*

Max found a glass and a pitcher on the desk and poured Wren a glass of water. "When my sister died, I went on a bender. I drank all the booze in the house. I was a mess. All I could think of was that it was my fault she'd died." At the time, he'd had no idea her death would be the first of many. He'd wallowed for far too long, when he should have been there for the rest of his family.

Max handed the glass to Wren, who only stared at him.

"The truth was, it was her choice. She felt called to help the sick of the town. And she did until she caught the sickness and died. I went to her then. For her, I would brave the risk of getting sick." Regret and anger and a small amount of acceptance tightened his chest. He couldn't what-if. He had to deal with his reality, which was completing his mission and getting back to his wife.

"What's your point?" Wren took the offered glass and sipped.

Max shook his head to dispel the memories. All he really knew was that Wren thought Serene helped his sister leave. He wished again he would've asked about Alesia and Wren's relationship on the walk here.

If they were like humans, it could be that Wren's sister was like his sister and wanted to make her own decisions. Max's sister hadn't talked to him when he hadn't supported her. Was that what had happened? He had to take the chance. "Your sister has made a choice you don't agree with. She hasn't died from it."

"Yet." Wren ground out, sounding stubborn and yet protective.

"Wouldn't you rather be there to help her when she needs it?"

Wren grumbled something.

"What?"

"Human, you don't understand."

Maybe it was more complicated than Max knew. Maybe Wren's sister had done something unforgivable.

"Is your sister dead to you right now?" Max asked. "Did her choice make you never want to forgive her?"

"No."

"Then quit acting like she's dead. She's not."

Wren's head snapped back as if Max had struck him. He slumped into the chair.

Max would wait to see what Wren had to say. He watched emotions play across Wren's face, but wasn't sure what they meant.

A few minutes later, Serene came back into the room trailed by two of Wren's people and the two guards who had been at the door.

"The bath is ready." Serene glanced between the two men and then pressed her lips together.

Max knew his time with Wren was up. He had either convinced him or ruined his chance. The silence made Max think he'd blown it. His jaw ached from keeping quiet. Nothing he could say at this point would help.

The two guards helped Wren stand and led him from the room.

"I delayed as long as I could. Did you convince him? They are all very worried about him." Serene leaned out the door to watch Wren's progress.

"Probably not." Max paced restlessly. He was too restless to even pick up a book. Everything hinged on a drunk helping them out. He ran his hand through his hair. "Is there some other way to get back my memories?"

Serene hesitated and sat in the chair Wren had been in. "Maybe. Wren is extremely knowledgeable and well connected in the magic community. If he doesn't know how to do it himself, he'll know someone who does. Without Wren on our side..." Serene tugged her hair and then shook her head.

The ache in Max's chest got worse.

"We can go up in ten minutes." Serene walked to the window and looked down. She rubbed her hand up and down her arm absently. She looked to be in deep thought.

He closed his eyes and took a breath. Perhaps he hadn't lost the chance yet. If he had guessed right about Alesia's situation, Wren might still help him. "So, what happened with Alesia?"

"Wren and Walter were best friends. Alesia left the tower to be with Walter," Serene said.

So, Wren didn't approve of the relationship? "Why?"

"Walter is part of the lizard-folk."

Max wasn't sure why that was a problem. But maybe lizard-folk and Aeros were enemies. But that wouldn't explain how Walter and Wren were best friends. Was this a species thing? Like a Romeo and Juliet romance?

Serene chuckled sadly. "She's also a princess."

The old-time royalty he'd read about in books had to marry for the state. They had very little control over who they ended up married to. "So, she gets an arranged marriage?"

"Oh no, she can choose her mate."

Then what was the issue? Wren must like Walter, or they wouldn't be friends and if Alesia was allowed to choose her own mate, what could be the dilemma? There was a piece of the puzzle he clearly didn't understand. He ran his hand through his hair in frustration. "Then what's the problem?"

Serene sighed and rubbed her eyes. "Alesia is special and very important to her people. I don't know much, but it has to do with her Grandmother." The answer was vague but left him feeling like there was something else about Alesia Serene didn't want to talk about.

The door slammed open. Max jumped to face them. Wren must be back with his verdict. Max would find out if Wren would help him.

"It's my sister you are talking about." Wren's voice snarled and his head crest stood at full height, which made him look like pictures of a cockatoo. He smelled cleaner and seemed to be in new clothing as well.

Max wasn't cowed; this was important to Max. Under the anger, Wren was hurt. "So you don't trust the guy?" Max asked.

"I trust Walter with my life." Wren stormed into the room. His eyes looked crazed enough to attack.

Max took half a step away before he lifted his chin and straightened his spine. If he backed down now, he would never get Wren to help him.

"Wren is very protective of his sister." Serene made calming motions with her hands.

"It sounds like he doesn't want her to be happy." Max thought he'd said it softly enough not to be heard, but Wren whipped out his long sword. He swayed on his feet, but he looked grim.

Fear soured Max's stomach and made his heart race. Even with Wren drunk, Max doubted he would survive a sword fight, even if he had a sword. He'd never had any training, not like Rose had.

Serene backed up. "We'll leave." She said it quickly and soothingly.

This was it. If he couldn't get through to Wren, Max was dead. "After this is all over, if you want to have a duel to the death, I'm in. Right now, I have to do my duty to my people. You should understand that."

"After this is all over, if you want to have a duel to the death, I'm in. Right now, I have to do my duty to my people. You should understand that." Wren breathed in and out for a full minute. His crest slowly lowered. "I'll hold you to that." Another minute passed, and Wren put the sword back into its sheath.

Max let out a relieved breath.

"What do you need?" Wren asked.

"We need you to magically restore Max's memories," Serene said.

A strange look passed over Wren's face. He slowly sank into the chair behind his desk. "Tell me what's going on first."

Max wasn't sure what to make of the request, but he'd give his full history and everything else if it would convince Wren to help him.

Serene took over and told Wren what Max had told her about Hope, the shield, the wizards, and the mission.

A guard came in and handed Wren a piece of paper.

Wren read it and didn't seem to be listening.

Max knew he should hold his temper in check. Mistress Yaneli had said that without Rose, the plan wouldn't work. If he alienated Wren, the only person they knew who could help them with his memory loss, he would surely have failed. He didn't even need the memories, he needed a way to complete his mission and see his Eleanor again.

Max watched Wren's face. He looked cold and distant, as if nothing ever affected him. Which was funny considering that not ten minutes ago, Wren had been a mess of wretchedness. Even after the bath Wren had taken, Max could still smell traces of honey.

Serene continued to feed Wren details. Even Max had lost the thread of what Serene was talking about, and it was his story.

He wished he knew this world better or had something he could offer in trade to make Wren a more willing participant. But nothing came to mind. The only thing he had was honesty.

Serene stopped talking, and Wren said nothing. He shuffled papers. What was he waiting for?

Serene glanced at Max. Her lips were pulled into a grim line. Was she expecting him to say something, or was she disappointed that Wren wasn't responding?

The silence stretched on until the whole room seemed to vibrate with Wren's intention not to help.

Something about the way Wren sat made Max think he wanted the fight now. For all his words, Wren wanted to take his anger and frustration out on someone. Max had volunteered to be that target. Perhaps if he agreed to fighting now, while Wren was drunk, he'd have a shot at making it a draw. Max sighed. "We can fight now."

"No." Serene said. "You both agreed to delay."

"He's only going to give us half-assed answers. He's not actually going to help us solve the problem. He probably even realized something. What we want is not going to aid us, or he has some other piece of information that changes the picture drastically. And then he'll do exactly as we ask of him and will giggle inside that he tricked us."

Wren stood and smirked. "I don't giggle."

Damn, I am right. "You *do* know something."

Wren drew his sword and tilted his head. "I think I do." He said this while still smirking.

Max bit back a curse. If he was this much of a jerk, no wonder his sister left.

Serene made a frustrated sound.

Wren obviously loved and missed his sister and was worried about her. But for some reason that wasn't enough to fix whatever their issue was. What could Max trade that Wren would want? Wren was a leader of his people. He had servants. Max knew nothing about Wren's sister's situation that could help. But it was worth a try.

"How about we make some kind of trade?" Max said evenly.

"Saving all the people you love must be worth a lot," Wren said blandly. He must know he held all the cards.

Max's mouth dried. There had to be something he could do.

"It is." He lifted his head, dreading what Wren would ask of him. It didn't matter. He would pay what was required. He remembered Mistress Yaneli saying he might never be able to come back. Now he recognized the truth of her words. He might have to give his life for those he loved and for the town he grew up in. If that's what it took for Eleanor to be saved, he'd do it. "But I think it's the same as how you value your sister."

Wren hesitated. Had Max struck a chord? "What did you have in mind?"

A small bubble of hope warmed Max at Wren's words. Wren thought there might be a way of helping him. Maybe he did want to go to his sister, but couldn't. "I can be your intermediary."

Wren raised his brows. "You think I would trust you for that?"

"Yes, because I can be trusted. When my issue is cleared up, I'll come and help you any way I can." Giving an open promise to a mage was epically stupid, but what choice did Max have?

"You are a terrible negotiator," Serene muttered and threw herself back into Wren's chair. "Why don't you guys sit?"

"I am not going to put my people at risk to make a better deal," Max said. Especially Eleanor, he added mentally. He sat down next to Serene. That left Wren standing. He walked stiff legged to a chair, but didn't sit down.

"You remind me of Alesia." Wren put his hand on the back of the chair. "I can't help you with your memories, but I have someone visiting from the Southern District who can give you what you need."

Even though Wren's expression didn't change, Max still felt like he was being tricked. He had to hope it would all turn out okay.

"Thank you," Max said.

Wren nodded carefully as if moving hurt. He tried to mask it, but Max had been there.

"Who is here? Are you having a council meeting?" Serene asked.

"That is her business," Wren said. He said in such a way it was clear he knew and had no intention of telling. Perhaps his reason for not telling had to do with his sister. Although why he would be drunk if he had a guest who might help Alesia made no sense.

Serene's eyes narrowed, but she said nothing.

Wren led them down two flights of stairs. When they reached the bottom, Serene scooted close to Max and whispered. "If she's on this floor, she's either very powerful or a friend."

Max hoped she was powerful. He couldn't imagine it was easy to get memories back.

Wren glanced at Serene and smiled. Even though the pull of his lips seemed sarcastic, it was the first smile he had shown Max and Serene since they'd arrived. "Or both," Wren said.

They walked down the bright open hall. Large windows showcased the blue sky and warm sun, making the tile glitter. Max felt lighter and let himself enjoy the beauty. If he could get his memories back, he would finally make progress on seeing Eleanor.

Wren led them down a hall to a plain wooden door. He brushed his hand across the front of his shirt and stood straighter. Then he knocked formally.

A moment later, a short, dark-haired woman with pale blue eyes opened the door. "Can I help you?"

"Valeria, may I introduce Max and Serene." At Serene's name the woman's eyes widened just slightly. Did she know Serene?

"May we come in?" Wren asked.

The woman stepped back into the room. She glanced at Wren and then invited them in. A small dart of hope fluttered in Max's chest. Perhaps she would help him.

The room was just as open and airy as the hallway. A curtain fluttered, drawing his gaze to the view of the city spilling out below them. The room confirmed she must be well respected. The furniture was solid and fancy with ornate carvings.

Dominating the middle of the floor were two swirling circles made of gold lines. It looked like a wheel with spokes connecting the outside ring to an inner smaller ring. The outer ring had six cushions resting in openings in the design.

"Please pick a cushion and sit," Valeria said.

How odd. She didn't even ask what Max's issue was. He glanced at Serene for guidance.

She hesitated. "The last time I sat in a spell circle was because my son was trying to figure out if something was contagious. Why do I feel the same way now?"

Max realized Serene was doing her best to look out for him.

"You will have to humor Valeria. I vouch for her." Wren sat on the light blue cushion.

"I know she's trustworthy, or she wouldn't be in this tower. I'd like to know what she's looking for with this spell circle," Serene said, crossing her arms. The tilt of her chin communicated her stubbornness on this point. Max wondered why she was worried.

"I am checking you for riders and other forms of possession," Valeria said. "Please sit, and I will answer your questions."

A spell circle? What was a rider? And why would she check for possession? Did she mean like evil spirits?

"Do I need to be careful of the lines?" Serene asked.

"No need," Valeria answered. She went to a desk in the corner and picked up a bag and a candle. Then she sat on a brown cushion next to Wren. She set her bag in her lap and the candle in an open space within reach of her cushion. She looked calm and collected. Max didn't get any odd feelings. If it would help his wife, he would do it.

Serene nodded and sat on the red cushion across from Wren.

That left Max the choice of a pink, a purple, or a gold cushion. None of them felt right. The choice that he made might be significant. He'd been the focus of spells before and knew that people being comfortable was important. He didn't want to sit on any of the cushions.

"May I remove the cushion and sit on the floor?" he asked.

Valeria nodded her permission. He chose the spot directly across from Valeria and next to Serene. He picked up the cushion and set it aside and sat in the spot before he could worry that it was the wrong thing to do.

He looked at Valeria who watched him as she pulled a silk-covered package out of her bag. Valeria nodded and then closed her eyes. When she opened them again, her eyes glowed a faint green. "I have never had an undead in my spell circle before."

Wren and Valeria looked at Max with murder in their eyes.

10

ROSE

Rose retraced her steps back to the front gate of the cemetery. A cemetery with its undead missing. She knew Joshua was nearby even if she couldn't see him.

With the amulet on, now that she was aware of the voices, she could still feel them pressing. They were farther away, but she could hear their whispers. *"Help us."*

The gate opened. Calder stood by the building where they'd left him. He nodded as they came out. "Find anything?" He had his hands behind his back. He looked relaxed, but a faint taint of fear and anger colored his smell. Why would he be angry? Perhaps he didn't like the city council sending other agents.

Joshua walked toward Calder. "We didn't."

"Help us. Free us." The voices whispered again. More and more voices joined the first. They filled her head. Fear trickled down her back. The voices were back. She took a deep breath

and tried to push them away, but nothing worked. Maybe if she shut the gate, that would help drown them out.

Rose closed the gate, ignoring the sting to her hands, and waited for relief. If the voices were from the cemetery, then closing the gate should block them out.

The voices didn't disappear. They weren't in the cemetery. She glanced around, puzzled, then down.

They were below her in the ground like a colony of ants.

She hung back behind Joshua, shivering. What was causing the voices? Why were they suddenly worse? She resisted the urge to cover her ears. Was she going crazy? Her stomach dropped as if she'd swallowed a headstone.

"Thanks again for letting us look around," Joshua said.

"No problem." Calder took back the amulets. "Will you be back?"

"The council is very busy." Joshua looked away, giving every impression of being bored with the conversation. Someone who didn't know him would have no idea that Joshua was watching for a reaction to gauge how much the other person knew. Joshua hadn't lied. He had dodged the question.

Calder pushed his hand through his hair. "I understand. I will make sure this stays under control."

Joshua nodded, walking toward her. They left quickly. She should've been relieved leaving Calder's speculative gaze, but the weight of the voices nagged at her.

She wouldn't discuss her impressions until they were out of enemy territory. That would mean away from the marks on the windows.

Once they were across the river, Joshua paused to see if they were being followed. He asked, "What do you think?"

"He seemed genuinely worried about the people." She rubbed her temple. The voices were still there. Moving away from the cemetery hadn't helped.

"He didn't want us to come back," Joshua said absently, and he cast a look at her she couldn't interpret.

"Think that's important?"

"Maybe. Even if he was sent by the council, few want the council sending back-up. Most would rather handle their situations themselves."

Rose shivered. A mental image of a gravestone and dark walls flashed in her mind. The feeling of being hemmed in pulsed through her. Desire to be free sped her heart and made her lightheaded. *Help us...*

Joshua's arms were around her, supporting her weight, and his face looked tense. "Rose?"

She blinked and the images receded to the back of her mind. A chorus of *"help us"* chanted in the back of her head. There must be a thousand different voices. She shivered again as she tried to regain her balance.

"I'm taking you to Master Phil's." Joshua picked her up and carried her down the alley.

Rose stiffened. Joshua hadn't carried her before, but she didn't have the energy to resist him.

"No, take me to Glenn." She rubbed her eyes. The voices were heavy, weighing her down and making it hard to think. They'd never been this bad before.

"Where is he?" Joshua's voice was sharp and urgent.

"West District." Her thoughts clouded. There was a reason that wasn't a good idea. "He's almost never in his shop, but I have a potion from him back at my room."

"You still live in my old house?" Joshua asked. It was the only place she'd lived since crossing out of Hope.

"Yes. I can walk." She hesitated, because of the worry on his face. She felt the need to reassure him. "It's never been this bad before."

He set her down and watched her carefully. "Tell me more." His voice was gentle.

She held on to his arm and tested her balance. She was still a little woozy.

"I get these weird visions and can hear voices in my head." She wasn't sure why she was worried. She'd already told him about being undead. And he had shared some of his own secrets. Remembering that made her feel less nervous.

"Are they real?"

That wasn't what she'd expected. Rose laughed and then stopped when she realized he was serious. She'd always assumed they were hallucinations, and she'd worked to ignore them. When that hadn't worked, she'd sought help. They did feel real. "They might be. At least they feel real."

"Once we get somewhere safer, let's see if we can find out."

The idea of having Joshua help her with something so personal was still startling, but it filled her with affection for him.

The trip back to her room took far longer than she'd expected. She felt as if she had been running. Her body was heavy and lethargic as she and Joshua walked to her little place off of the main market. It was a first-floor room, behind one of the few restaurants. The heavy aroma of spices and cooking food permeated the air. She didn't even stop to enjoy the smell. She wanted to get inside and sit down.

She opened her door. The room seemed to shrink in size when Joshua walked in. He closed and bolted the door behind them.

The room spun. She sat down on her chair with a thump. Everything felt heavy. Fatigue and the voices pulled at her senses. She just needed a rest.

He gazed around the room. "There's no bed." His eyes fell on the block of wood she was in the middle of carving. It was a tall tree with branches, flowers, and leaves. Hundreds of tiny faces peered out between the foliage. Only some of the figures were human. The tree was six feet tall and three feet wide. She'd started at the bottom and had been slowly making her way to the top. The design was now an inch from the top.

"Did you make this?" Joshua picked up one of the knives that she'd left on the table.

She nodded. Her cheeks heated with embarrassment. She'd never shown her work to anyone before.

He frowned and seemed to debate with himself. "Where is the potion?"

Rose hated taking the potion. It did push the voices away, but made her feel so weird. She pointed to the cabinet.

He pulled out a simple sealed bottle. "It's the last one."

"I'll have to send word to Glenn at his shop that I need more," she said absently, staring at the bottle as Joshua brought it to her. The dark glass seemed menacing.

She popped off the top and couldn't help the sniff. She knew she made a face. The potion never smelled good. They all tended to smell like rotting fish, but the desire to push away the voices overrode her revulsion. She held her nose and chugged the bottle as fast as she could.

Joshua watched her, looking concerned.

She shuddered against the taste and swallowed against the revulsion. She focused on keeping the fluid down. The shudder this time wasn't fear.

After a moment, the voices dimmed. A calm settled over her. She took a deep breath, feeling separated from her body. She slumped back against the chair. Relief lightened her chest.

Joshua put the top back on and put the potion in his bag. "Feeling better?"

"Yes." Her lips felt a bit numb. That was new. "The voices

aren't gone. The potion just pushes them a-away." Her numb lips stumbled on the last word.

The world now held the slight gray tinge she got after a potion. The odd taste still coated the inside of her mouth. "I just need a few minutes."

"How long have you been hearing voices?" His voice held an off tone. His eyes looked grim. She'd never seen him quite this way. It worried her that she didn't understand why he looked so grim.

She knew he was just trying to help, but it was hard to get past her reluctance to share. "As long as I've been here." It started off with a single voice. Over time, they multiplied. Glenn's potions had pushed the voices away.

Joshua blurred. Rose clenched her hands. She'd waited too long before taking the potion. This episode had snuck up on her. She'd taken a dose a few days ago. It should have lasted for a week. Worry pooled in her gut. There must be something wrong with her.

Joshua blinked at her and then sat down near her. "Do you remember the first day we met?"

Rose focused on his eyes. The rest of his face wouldn't quite come into view, but his eyes were gentle. "Yes."

Her mind went back to that day. Joshua had been very kind to her then. She'd been so lost and alone. Rose glanced at her friend, and her throat closed. "Why did you help me?"

Joshua held her gaze. "I remembered being adrift and alone in a strange town, having lost everything and not being sure what to do."

"And someone helped you?" she whispered.

Joshua laughed, but it had an edge of sadness to it. "No. I always wished someone had." She couldn't imagine what it must have been like to have no one. He had made everything so much easier for her.

"I know I haven't always been the best friend, but I'm here for you now," Joshua said.

That he was doubting their friendship annoyed her. Mostly because she knew it was her fault. She could choose to change that in the next moment. He waited.

"Hope is a town of mages. It was protected during the Merge by a set of brothers married to a set of sisters."

He nodded.

She continued despite the fear that skittered up and down her back. "I was married and had two daughters. I wasn't magical, but that didn't matter. Then a plague hit." She rubbed at the ache in her chest.

"How did you get here?"

"When my husband and children died, the matron of the town asked me to take my stone to an ally on the other side of the shield. He would help take down the shield, which she said would rid the town of the plague. I-I lost the stone right after crossing and never met the ally."

"How did you get to be undead?"

"I have no idea." She still didn't. She'd gone to a healer to ask about no longer needing sleep. He'd been the one to tell her that anything living had to sleep. The rest had come to her slowly. She'd needed to find out what it meant to be undead in a way that didn't reveal she was researching herself. She'd been careful not to betray her secret to anyone she talked to. She'd even given the HPA samples of her own body. It hadn't helped.

Joshua squeezed her shoulder. "Where is Hope?"

"I don't know." She was lying to him and herself. The fear had a direction to it. She could be spun in a circle and would always know the direction Hope was in.

He watched her. "You're scared."

She *was* scared and had always been terrified of going back. "I never want to go back." Her voice cracked on the last word.

He nodded. "Tell me about the voices. Maybe I can send a soul wisp out."

She closed her eyes and pushed away the fear to focus on the voices. "I-it's a chorus."

"Which direction?" His voice was gentle and persistent.

"I don't know. Everywhere? Nowhere?" She shivered. The room felt cold. "Mostly down."

"Are there some below us now?"

Rose listened, trying to pull apart the feeling, but she couldn't focus. "Not right here. Closer to the river? Maybe?" She wasn't sure.

She closed her eyes. It felt good to lie back. She could drift for a while.

Joshua tapped her shoulder. "Let's get back to Master Phil's."

She stood, and the room swayed. They were all supposed to meet back at Daniel's, she remembered.

"Maybe he'll know." Joshua's voice sounded odd.

She leaned against the doorframe to stop the swaying. Through the haze she realized she might not be able to make it that far.

11

MAX

<u>Afternoon, Primum second, 300 years post-Merge</u>

The scent of fear invaded Max's senses. Wren and Valeria looked at him from the other side of the spell circle like he was a thing to be eliminated.

The word undead echoed in Max's ears. Confusion rose, swamping his body with heat. How could he be an undead? Valeria had to be wrong.

"He doesn't know." Serene's voice was calm, but strong. It only added to his confusion. Had Serene known he was undead this whole time?

Max swiveled to look at Serene. The expression on her face reminded him of his mom when the other boys had teased him about having no magic. Serene had the same kindness toward him and urged him to accept who he was the same as his mother had. Confusion and panic filled his belly and chest. He wasn't undead. He'd know if he was. Wouldn't he?

"How is that possible?" Wren demanded.

"What are you talking about? I'm not undead," Max said. He wasn't undead. He was a living person from Hope. He had a wife, Rose, nieces, friends, and a mission.

Valeria turned to face him, looking thoughtful. "May I see your hand?"

Max hesitated. She seemed nice enough, but there was power in the way she held herself. This could be a trap.

He could try to leave the Rookery. He thought about the guards and the stairs. It would be a long, bitter battle against skilled fighters if they wanted him to stay. He had no fighting skills. And it would mean abandoning Serene. He couldn't abandon his new friend. He wasn't that kind of person, and he had no way of finding Rose in a city this size. And he still didn't have his memories. He'd never be able to see Eleanor without them.

He sighed and held his hand out to Valeria.

She took his hand and grasped it firmly, holding on to his thumb and pinky as if she expected him to yank it away. She closed her eyes and murmured something. A line of concentration showed on her forehead, but her grip didn't shift.

"You have missing memories?" The monotone of her voice sent a shiver down his spine. He'd heard that tone when master mages cast spells. She was doing powerful magic on him.

Rose had been here five years, and he'd left Hope only a few days after her. He must have been here. He wasn't sure what it all meant. "Yes, I guess I've been here five years. I only remember crossing over," Max said quietly. He thought he saw sympathy in her expression.

"Would you say you are driven to save Hope?" The words had an underlying tingle of magic. They must be a key phrase to her spell.

"Wouldn't you be?" Max blinked. Her words implied he had something controlling him. That he was undead and under someone's control. That maybe his missing memories were related. A strange sense of hope fluttered in his belly. She might be able to return his memories. If she did, he still had a chance to complete the mission and see Eleanor.

"What did you think there?" Valeria asked.

"A-about my wife, Eleanor," Max said.

Valeria nodded, and a pleased smile flitted across her face. He had no idea why. She closed her eyes and murmured words he couldn't quite hear.

His thoughts spiraled like the glass pieces in a kaleidoscope. Serene seemed to know he was undead. He shuddered. How had he turned into an evil monster without his knowledge? Fear and anger bubbled up from his belly. He didn't feel any different. But he must be different.

When Valeria's eyes opened, he asked, "What does it mean if I am undead? Will I turn into a zombie or a skeleton and attack the town? Am I a danger to others?" He kept his gaze on Valeria. For the first time, he noticed the tattooed symbols on her hands. They were drawn in a reddish-brown color and extended up to her sleeve. Tattoos filled in on her face as he watched. The tattoos hadn't been there before the spell. They, too, exuded a shiver of magic.

The symbols shimmered as he looked upon them. Resisting the strong urge to stroke the symbols that appeared, he jerked his hand back. She held on, proving she was far stronger than she looked.

"Why did you jerk your hand away?" There was an edge to her voice he didn't understand.

He could feel color flood his face. "I want to trace the symbols. See how many you have. Touch each one." The words came out before he could catch them and left him embarrassed. What he spoke of wasn't desire for her as a woman but desire to be close to the symbols painted onto her skin.

Valeria stared at him as if deciding whether he spoke the truth. He didn't know if he passed her test or not, but she released his hand. The symbols faded, but he couldn't look away from her face. This must be part of the spell. His mouth dried with worry. He sensed that her judgment would decide his fate in this world.

"I have good news, strange news, and bad news," Valeria announced. She leaned back and he was able to look away.

Relief made him giddy. The spell was over. This was his judgment. His heart beat wildly, and he forced himself to look at Serene and Wren.

"What's the good news?" Serene asked.

"Max is not evil," Valeria said.

Max jerked back to look at Valeria. Surprise added to the confusion in his chest. That was the good news? It wasn't that he wasn't undead, but that he wasn't evil.

"Even if he was an ass, I sensed he was trying to help me." Wren brushed the feathers on his neck absently, which gave the impression he was deep in thought.

"What does it mean 'not being evil?'" Serene asked.

"Evil is the ultimate of being self-centered. No one else matters. No one else's desires, wants, or needs matter. Anyone could be sacrificed for what the evil person desires." Valeria pulled another item from her bag and unwrapped it carefully. She kissed the gray and gold stone and placed it on a space next to her.

Max shivered. She was preparing to do even more powerful magic. He'd seen the tokens the mages wore in Hope and the items the mages kept on necklaces so they would always be prepared for a spell.

The bad news was probably that he was undead, but what could the strange news be? That was the news that seemed the scariest. "What's the strange news?" Max asked.

"You are undead, but of a kind I've never encountered," she said. "Life is fueled by positive energy. It grows and connects. The undead are usually created from negative energy. It keeps a body in a state it is not meant to be in. Most undead seek life energy to feed the negative energy."

Dismay and regret pulsed through him. There was no way he would feed on life energy to stay alive. That would be murder. He would have to figure out how to get his mission done and end his own not-life.

Valeria unwrapped another item from her bag, a blue, silk-covered button, kissed it, and placed it on another open space. Perhaps she was preparing a spell that would kill him. The easy way she held herself made that seem unlikely, but maybe she was just a good actress. Fear, regret, and anger swirled in his chest.

He looked between Wren and Serene. Neither one said anything. It was as if they wanted him to ask the questions. He took a breath, fighting down the dread slowly building in his chest.

"Then what am I?"

"You are undead, but your body is still being fueled by positive energy."

Confusion fluttered through him. Weren't all undead evil? If he wasn't based on evil, then what did being undead mean? Could he have a life as an undead? Max wasn't sure how to feel about being undead. He didn't think that Valeria would say he wasn't evil just to be nice. And he didn't think that she would make stuff up. "How do you know?"

She seemed to debate what to say. "The tattoos you saw are a blessing. They were made specifically to keep evil out. You were able to touch me with no pain. In fact, they drew you. Only positive energy can stand to be near my tattoos."

A small wisp of hope entered his chest. If he was made of

positive energy, maybe it wouldn't be so bad to be an undead. Maybe he wasn't fated to lose parts of himself and eat his friends.

"What spell are you casting? I don't recognize the pattern," Wren asked, interrupting Max's thoughts.

"Keep watching and see if you can figure it out." Valeria unwrapped another object, which, this time, was a tangled ball of purple yarn, and placed it in the last open spot.

"I thought wizards needed to concentrate while casting a spell," Serene said.

Max realized they were giving him time with his thoughts. Space to think about what it all meant. But he was stuck in a loop. He was undead but not evil. If he was undead, he must be evil. Everything he had ever seen had portrayed the undead as evil, malevolent scourges. So, did that mean he was not *really* undead?

"I'm not casting the spell now. I'm setting the spell up. Besides, I'm a witch, not a wizard," Valeria said.

The word witch caught Max's attention. There were no witches in Hope. Witches had a mixed reputation as devil worshipers. She was in some ways just like Max.

"What's the difference between a witch and a wizard?" Serene asked.

Max wondered the same. Would Valeria admit to devil worship?

"It's in how they approach magic," Valeria said.

"A wizard holds the magic outside of his or her body. They use objects as carriers. Their emotions get in the way of magic. It's about control and logic," Wren said.

Valeria grinned. "Whereas witches have their magic inside. Both schools are about control. Witches use objects to evoke feelings that fuel the spell."

"A wizard isn't trained to use their emotions as fuel. If their emotions are involved, the magic will act in unexpected ways," Wren said, but he wasn't using his previous tone. He seemed distracted and focused on what Valeria was doing. Max wondered if that was another clue about their relationship? He had agreed to help Wren, so maybe he'd better pay attention.

"And witches can't create spells for things they don't believe in. If they can't access their feelings, or if they're lying to themselves, the magic won't work correctly, if it works at all." Valeria added.

The wizards in Hope had always seemed so in control. Sometimes almost robotic. Most of them didn't seem to feel deeply about anything. Was what he knew about witches and undead wrong?

"So, the reputation of witches gaining power from devils isn't true?" Max asked.

Valeria paused and her gaze went to his. "For some witches that is true." A knowing smile touched her lips. "The same way that only some undead are evil."

Busted. He smiled back at her, recognizing that they were kindred spirits. They were both good when it would have been expected they'd be bad.

Valeria lit the candles within arm's length, which drew his gaze back to the swirl of lines on the floor. Serene had said the lines were for a spell circle. "Figured out what I'm doing?" Valeria's voice was teasing.

"Not at all." Wren shook his head and looked frustrated. "Your spell components make no sense."

Valeria pointed to the tangled ball of purple yarn. "This has emotional meaning to me. I use it to seek the truth."

"Why yarn?" Wren asked. "I would have used something pure like salt or perhaps water."

The Hope wizards carried bags of salt and pure water, depending upon what they specialized in.

"This yarn was with me when I went through my own truth finding. It has come to feel like the knots we tie ourselves into. The mix of truth and lies we all tell ourselves. It represents confusion."

"So I would need to find objects with emotional meaning if I were to become a witch?" Wren asked.

Max wasn't sure what Wren was talking about. But Valeria raised a brow at Wren, and his mouth snapped shut. His face went red.

"You still haven't told us about the bad news," Serene pointed out.

"Just a moment." Valeria closed her eyes and stilled. Her movements became controlled. She spoke in a language Max hadn't heard and didn't sound like the words the mages in Hope used. The faint scent of cinnamon and the distant echoes of bells ringing brought chills up his spine.

A golden globe of magic appeared before Valeria. Max jerked back. The tingle of magic from the globe felt innocent, almost child-like.

Valeria said something else in her strange language.

The golden ball shimmered and sank into the lines of the spell circle. The lines glowed and created a thin barrier that looked like the soap bubble he had crossed to get out of Hope, except with a golden hue that rose around them.

Serene's soft sound of surprise turned Max's gaze. She paled and her lips pressed together.

"Nicely done." Wren looked at the shield and cocked his head back and forth.

"Max?" Valeria asked.

He shifted to look at her.

The tattoos were back, covering her body. "Will you let me help you?" Valeria asked.

Except in the most dire circumstances, anyone good asked

for permission before doing a spell. The mages in Hope had all made that clear.

"What will you do?" he whispered.

"Ask you questions and then reveal the truth to you."

Max still didn't know the bad thing. "The bad thing?"

She nodded. "And then help you, if you want help with the bad thing."

He swallowed back his fear. Truth could be a hard thing, but having her help him deal with it eased some of the tension in his gut. Wren had never said what she specialized in. Perhaps she would be able to restore his memories. The first step in seeing Eleanor. He nodded.

"How do you feel about Hope?"

This question was easy. "I still need to save them. If I do, I can see Eleanor again." He felt this through his soul.

"How do you feel about Eleanor?"

His feelings for Eleanor were strong. He'd known her his whole life and had loved her for most of it. Joy lightened his chest; it had been the happiest moment of his life when he'd asked her to marry him and she'd said yes.

Serene gasped as if he had said those words aloud. Max couldn't look away from Valeria.

"How did you become undead?" Valeria asked.

He had no answer. He still didn't quite believe he was undead. He felt a pull, like little threads were coming out of his fingers, toes, and head. "I don't know."

"I see the spell has a truth component to it," Wren said.

At Wren's tone, annoyance filtered through Max. "Why don't you tell us why you and Alesia have a problem?"

Valeria lifted her hand. "Please. Before we fight. You must know there is some element of control on you. Something is driving you to seek Hope. It's using the energy of your feelings for Eleanor as a power source. Right now, it is goading you to fight."

Her words stilled the growing anger in his chest. "I don't understand."

"The control element might be what's holding you together as an undead. You may die if I break that bond."

He gasped and panic flared, sending shivers up his back. He was afraid he would die before returning to Hope. He closed his eyes. He took a slow breath, fighting down the panic the thought of dying before he could save Eleanor brought. The best course to get to Hope was to let Valeria remove the control. The thought calmed him and pushed back the fear.

"Do you think removing the control element will kill me?"

"I have never seen an undead such as yourself, so I have no idea what might cause you to die."

"Beheadings and stakes to the heart are generally bad no matter what energy animates your body," Wren said.

"That works on birds too," Max said.

Wren smirked. "Why are you involved, Serene?"

"Joshua and I got word from Alesia to protect Rose," Serene said. "Alesia foresaw the need." Her eyes widened as if she hadn't intended to confess that fact to Wren. The truth spell must affect everyone in the circle.

"You never told me that." Wren's crest rose and his neck feathers fluffed, but his eyes conveyed his hurt at her words.

"Remember how you said never to come back here again?" Serene asked sharply.

"And yet here you are!" Wren growled.

Wren and Serene looked ready to jump up and tussle. Worry their anger could break the spell and cost him his chance to see his wife sent a jolt of fear into Max's chest.

"The control element is trying to get us to fight," Valeria said calmly.

"The spell is manipulating us?" Wren asked, sounding much calmer. "Then removing the spell must be a good thing."

Serene looked at Wren. "I'm sorry I didn't tell you about Alesia. I hate seeing you two estranged. She misses you."

"I miss her as well. We can't be together until—"

"Hush, Wren, now is not the time." Valeria focused her attention back on Max. "What is it you wish to do?"

Max looked at the people in the circle with him. Valeria, the good witch, who watched him with patient compassion. Serene, who had a similar expression. She seemed offended that someone might try to control him. And Wren, who was hiding something. Something to do with his sister. Something to do with why he'd become friends with Valeria in the first place. Perhaps why he was trying to learn to be a witch.

Max realized if the spell was fighting so hard to prevent him from removing the control, then it must be good to remove it. "So, if I leave the spell alone, I may be a danger to my friends and family. If I attempt to have it removed, I might die?" He didn't like the idea of accidentally hurting Rose or anyone else because of a spell. He didn't want to die, but he also didn't want to be manipulated by magic.

Valeria nodded. "The control element could force you to hurt your friends and family."

"Please, do it." His voice came out a harsh croak.

Valeria closed her eyes and swayed to some internal rhythm. She spoke in a low voice and lifted her hands, spreading her fingers wide. The golden energy thickened around them, blocking the outside world.

A long, ragged cry echoed in the room. As the darkness pressed around him, he realized the scream was his.

12

ROSE

<u>Early evening, Primum second, 300 years post-Merge</u>

Rose drifted back to her body from the floating gray clouds. The scent of raw vegetables reassured her. When she detected Daniel and Joshua, she knew she was at Daniel's place. A feeling of peace stole over her. She was safe. She wasn't sure how she'd gotten here. Joshua had probably carried her.

She opened her eyes. Daniel's sitting room looked the same. The fireplace was to her left. She must be sitting in the rocking chair. A heavy blanket lay across her lap. On the little table next to her was the blue mug she'd used when she'd stayed here. Daniel had somehow known it was her favorite. The scent of chamomile drifted from the cup. She'd never been his patient before.

"W-what happened?" she asked.

"You passed out," Joshua said.

She could still feel the effects of the potion in her body. A distance, like a pool of water, lay between her and her skin. The voices were farther away, but still waiting at the edge of her perception. They hadn't been that near when she'd taken the previous doses. The voices were getting closer. Unease curled in her gut.

The clatter of a pan brought her attention to Daniel. He'd just set the pot on the flame. He cooked when he was worried. When she'd been trapped with him, he'd once made her a stew that had been the best she'd ever had. They had cut vegetables together and laughed.

Daniel glanced her way and said, "Drink the tea. It will help."

He moved to his table and the click of a knife said he was chopping onions. The taps seemed louder in the room. He was trying to give her some privacy. Her stomach warmed at the thought of him not only feeding her, but of him caring.

She took a careful sip of tea. The mug was only partially filled, and the fluid danced wildly in the cup as she lifted it to her mouth. "Something is wrong with me."

"What can I do?" Joshua asked.

"I can still hear them. The voices. They're farther away, but still there." She didn't like the crack at the end of her voice.

"We'll figure this out." Joshua patted her shoulder. "Try to rest."

She closed her eyes and relaxed into the chair. She was so at ease here. The sounds in the room became more pronounced. A second knife joined in chopping. Joshua had probably grabbed a knife to help Daniel cut vegetables.

"She's stabilized," Daniel said. "You said it was a potion that caused it?"

"I have the bottle. There's still a little fluid left at the bottom. Can that help us figure out what's going on?"

"Yes, that would help," Daniel said. His voice was almost lost in the chopping. "I'm really worried. She's reacting as if she's been poisoned."

Rose remembered all too clearly the vile taste of the potion and how she had felt afterward. Had it been poison?

"It didn't smell like poison that would affect a human, but with Rose being..." Joshua stumbled to a stop.

"When did you find out?" Daniel asked.

Joshua sighed. "She is only now trusting me."

"But she is trusting you. You are one of a very few who know her."

"Do I look like I need a pep talk?" Joshua's tone was wry.

"Yes, all part of my service."

Fondness for both men warmed her.

The movement of a chair and the sound of something getting plopped into the stew followed. She opened her eyes. Daniel walked back to Joshua who was sitting at the table. Daniel looked calm as he ambled across the room. But something about the set of his eyes and the way his mouth pulled just slightly down communicated his worry. A prick of guilt stabbed at her. She hadn't meant to worry him.

"Let me have the bottle, and I'll try to identify it." Daniel held out a hand.

Joshua took out the vial and handed it to Daniel. It was made of the same dark glass as Glenn's bottles. How had Joshua gotten it?

Daniel stepped closer to the window and held the vial to the light. He must be looking at the color. He lifted the stopper and wafted some of the scent to his nose and made a yuck face. Amusement slid through her. The brew must stink.

The air seemed heavy and the distance between her and her body was still there. She watched Daniel work. The precise way he held the bottle and the concentration showing on his face appealed to her. She found him attractive. It was unsettling to realize how short of a time they had known each other and yet how much she trusted him.

He put the vial in a rack on his work bench. He pulled out pouches and vials from the stand and drawers and added them to the bottle. One white powder sent up a plume of smoke. His shoulders bunched and his face set. He added something else, and a small spark erupted from the top of the flask. His mouth pulled down into a frown. He looked positively angry.

She closed her eyes, wondering what could make a man like Daniel angry. Her thoughts drifted and the lethargy claimed her.

A gentle hand shook her, and something pressed to her lips. The drop on her tongue caused liquid fire to burn down her throat in a warm wake to her stomach. The distance between her and her body reduced.

"This is the same potion you gave Max. I can taste the White Thorn." She opened her eyes and saw both Joshua and Daniel looking at her. They both wore expressions of concern. She hadn't thought she had let anyone close, but there they were, kneeling in front of her, with a shattered blue cup on the floor between them.

"Are you back with us?" Daniel asked.

She blinked, trying to understand his words. How had her favorite cup ended up on the ground? The last she remembered Joshua had been slicing veggies. The scent of stew was now heavy in the air. Did that mean it had been awhile? "What happened?"

"You were being poisoned," Daniel said, looking annoyed. "Why didn't you come to me?"

She looked at him. It had never occurred to her to have him look at what Glenn was giving her. What was wrong with her? Pressure built in her chest, her throat closed, and her eyes heated. "I'm sorry." As soon as the words were out, the faint feel of tears trickled down her face.

Both men had almost identical expressions of shock and dismay. Then she was caught in their embraces. A strange cocktail of embarrassment and affection made her shake.

After a few moments, she had to say something to break the tension. "I never thought I'd see you two hugging."

"Add it to the things you do for love," Joshua said, shrugging.

Love. Warm affection filled her chest. Yes, she loved both of these men, but in far different ways.

Daniel turned away, but she thought she saw a blush color his cheeks. "Tell me about this Glenn," Daniel demanded.

Reluctance and fear pooled in her belly. It seemed wrong to talk about Glenn. But these men were important to her. She'd just admitted to herself she loved them. "Why?"

"He tried to kill you!" Daniel spun back and raised his hands, looking exasperated.

"No, he would never do that. It must have been an accident," she protested.

"He knew what he was doing. No question with the ingredients that he used," Daniel muttered. "Nothing in that formula would help the living or the undead."

"How did you meet him?" Joshua pitched his voice to be low and soothing. Somehow it was easier to talk to Joshua.

"I've always known him," Rose said. The statement puzzled her. She tried to think about the first time she'd met Glenn, but came up with nothing. She didn't remember meeting him.

Joshua pulled up a chair. "Did we meet on your first day from Hope?"

The word Hope caused her heart to ratchet up. Fear crawled up her spine and lodged at the back of her neck. She took a deep breath, trying to calm her heart.

Daniel knelt beside her. He took her hand in his big warm one. "Is it just that word that makes you afraid?" He stroked his fingers up the back of her hand.

Rose shivered. The touch was both soothing and something more. She held his gaze for a moment before nodding.

"Did we meet on your first day in town?" Joshua asked.

She squeezed Daniel's hand. "Yes."

"Did you know him before you met me?"

"I...I?" She paused to think. She didn't know Glenn from before she crossed over, but after she had settled into Joshua's old place, she'd known his name, where he was, and had sought him out.

When she had walked into his shop he called her by name and had the potion ready for her. She hadn't had any money to give to him. He laughed and said it wasn't a problem. She didn't remember actually meeting him for the first time. Could she have missing memories like Max? "I don't remember how we met."

"Did you have a mission like Max?" Daniel asked.

"Not anymore." She didn't have a mission. The locket felt heavy around her throat. The souls of her dead children weighed on her. "It hurts too much to think about them."

"Who?" Joshua asked.

"My children." She pulled out the necklace.

"That's the necklace I found in the HPA stairway," Joshua said. "I thought you had died saving me from the HPA ambush."

She remembered the stairwell and leading the HPA agents away from Joshua. She had no idea how she lost the necklace, but Joshua had given it back to her later that night. Joshua must not have looked inside.

She opened the necklace and showed them the pictures inside. A vise grip wrapped around her heart and squeezed tight. She felt as if the grief for her children along with some other force were pulling at her.

The noises in the room faded. The sharp scent of fear filled her nose. The colors grayed. A ringing started from far away and got louder and louder.

The noise. The voices. The thumping of her heart. The tangled ball of emotions crushing her chest. It was all too much.

She covered her ears and screamed to drown it out.

13

MAX

<u>Early evening, Primum second, 300 years post-Merge</u>

Cold tile pressed against Max's left cheek. His skin tingled. The feel of three people hovering over him tickled against his senses. Senses he could admit for the first time he hadn't had before in Hope. A thrill shot through him. He felt as if he had shed ten layers of clothing.

Suddenly he realized he'd known where the zombies were earlier because he had smelled them. He'd heard them and seen them far faster than he would have when he lived in Hope. He'd been reading subtle cues from both Wren and Serene based on their scent and pulse.

He took a deep breath of cool, crisp air and sorted through the information the air carried. Serene was worried about him. They all were, even Wren.

He opened his eyes. The light was brighter. He rolled over to sit up, and his satchel caught on the floor for a moment.

Wren's feathers sparkled with colors just under the white surface, colors he'd never seen before.

"You lived," Valeria said, sounding relieved.

"You had me worried," Serene added, giving him a tentative smile. She helped him as he rose.

He felt a little unsteady, but could feel his strength returning.

"How do you feel?" Valeria asked.

"Much better. Much clearer." The yearning drive to get back to Hope at all costs was gone. He still wanted to help his people, but he didn't feel the impending doom hovering over him. His people were in trouble, and there was a deeper game afoot. But he might have friends who could help. He turned his attention to Valeria.

She watched him with an expression of curiosity. There was so much he didn't know. She'd been able to break the spell, but could she help him figure out why it was put on him in the first place? Surely more information would help Rose and Hope.

"Why would I have a control element?"

Valeria shrugged. "The fact you can ask that question now proves it's gone."

"You have a guess?" Wren asked into the quiet room.

"Unless the control is to stop murderous impulses, such a thing is generally evil. It manipulates the person in complete disregard for what they want or how they feel. Max's control was about going back to Hope."

"To see my wife, I had to find the stones and bring Rose," Max said. Dread twisted in his stomach. There was a memory at the edge of his mind. Something had happened that involved Eleanor.

Valeria pursed her lips in thought. "What about your missing memories?"

Max closed his eyes and tried to think back. "Not much, just gravestones and a sense of...pressure."

"You may remember with time." Valeria met Max's gaze. "A powerful mage cast the spell. An adept of the highest order. It was intricately and intimately constructed."

Was she hinting about something?

"Meaning the person knew Max?" Serene asked, looking puzzled.

"Or had plenty of time to get to know him under duress." Valeria picked up the items from her spell circle and put them away.

"I saw no indication he had been tortured," Wren said.

"Manipulation is far easier than actual physical torture." Her voice was gentle and her gaze focused on Wren. He grimaced.

Whatever was going on between the two wouldn't help Max. Since he owed Wren, it might come back and haunt him later. For now, he had to focus on what was in front of him. Hopefully, Rose and Joshua were back from the cemetery. Maybe they had found a clue as to what was really going on. Max stood up and offered his hand to Serene.

"Where do you think you're going?" Wren asked.

Max wasn't sure why Wren would want to know, but Max saw no reason not to answer. "Back to Master Phil's. Rose and Joshua are meeting us there."

Wren frowned. "I'm going with you."

"What? Why?" Serene asked.

Max welcomed the help, but now that the memories were a dead-end, what could Wren do for him?

"Alesia told you Rose should be protected. So, I'm going to help protect her." Max had heard the expression of ruffled feathers, but hadn't seen what it meant until now. The feathers on Wren's neck and chest puffed up.

Serene's mouth opened, and then she laughed a bit. "You would be a valued team member if you joined us." Her voice was soothing.

Max agreed. Having a wizard on their side would be a good thing. "Thank you."

"I'll come as well," Valeria said, surprising Max.

Wren glanced at Valeria and frowned. "I'm not sure that's a good idea."

Valeria seemed thoughtful. "It could help," she said softly. If Max hadn't been looking, he would have missed Wren's flinch.

Wren got up abruptly.

A little while later, Serene led them through town.

With his new awareness of his senses, he could tell when they entered Shifterville. There was a musk in the air and criss-crossed scent trails that led off to different communities.

He could hear faint yipping in the distance. A shifter family had a den up ahead and to the right. The kids must be playing. He listened with amusement to try to picture what the yip and mock snarls translated to in movement.

A scream of anguish broke his concentration. *Rose!* The sound twisted something deep within him, making him feel frantic.

He ran toward the scream, splashing through a puddle, pushing past a group of shifters, trying to reach her. The sound stopped, and he was able to breathe. The next crossing looked familiar, so he kept moving.

He rounded the corner, and the scream started again. Chills raced up his spine, and he sprinted down the alley. Where was the door?

The scream stopped abruptly, stopping his heart. Was Rose dead?

Master Phil's door was closed. Max grabbed the handle, pulled, and ripped the door off its hinges. He stared in shock at the door, then tossed it aside.

Inside, Rose was on the floor with her arms wrapped around her head.

She lifted her head, clenched her fists, and screamed as if she was being torn in half. He couldn't see any obvious source of her pain.

A shifting of air behind him had him whirling around. Valeria was there. "Break the necklace." she said, sounding calm.

Joshua lunged forward and pulled the necklace from around Rose's neck. It snapped off.

The change in Rose was immediate. She stood up in one slow motion. Relief filtered through him. He never wanted to hear Rose or anyone he loved scream like that again. "Rose?"

She turned toward the door, but her gaze stared past him. Her eyes and expression were blank.

Fear fisted his chest, making it hard to breathe. What was going on? Why was Rose acting this way? He glanced up at Joshua and Master Phil, who both looked shocked.

Rose charged to the door. Max stepped in front of her, and she walloped him. A fancy kick he hadn't seen coming left him sprawled on the floor. But that brief contact left the tingle of magic. It was the same feeling he'd had before Valeria had broken the spell that controlled him. It felt like the same sort of compulsion.

"Get out of her way!" Master Phil shouted.

Valeria and Wren dove aside, and Rose ran out the door.

"Follow her," Master Phil said.

Master Phil and Joshua jumped over Max and headed out the door.

Max stood up and followed them out. He sniffed the air. Her scent was gone.

14

MAX

Frustration boiled over Max. If Rose's scent was gone, he had no means to track her. Without knowing the city, he had no idea what direction to even try.

Master Phil's door that he'd ripped from the hinges was to his right. It taunted him. What good were these new powers if he couldn't even keep Rose safe?

"This is awkward," Valeria said. She stood in the middle of the alley looking small and alone.

Max had no idea what prowled in the night here. It seemed best to get them both inside. "Master Phil won't mind you coming in." Max hoped that was true.

Valeria went inside with him. They both stood facing the door.

"I don't know the city well enough to chase after her."

"That was probably wise," Valeria said, gently.

Hopefully the others could find Rose and bring her back. If she didn't want to come, there would be a heck of a fight.

The idea of Wren getting his butt kicked by Rose made Max chuckle. The amusement ended, leaving him feeling adrift. What if they couldn't find her?

The shadows moved and the scents shifted, but nothing approached the door. Which was good, since Max wasn't sure what he and Valeria would do if they were attacked.

A few minutes later, Wren walked back in and touched Valeria's arm. "Are you okay?"

She nodded.

"I scanned the area. I wasn't able to track her. Something hid her from my magical senses." Wren shook his head as if nothing like that had happened to him before.

Feeling like he should contribute something, Max said, "Her scent is gone as well."

Wren paced back and forth in front of the wrecked entrance.

Master Phil's house seemed so vulnerable with the gaping hole. "Can you help me fix this?" Max asked.

Wren nodded and helped him place the door back on its hinges. Wren whispered a spell that sent a tingle of reaction where Max touched the wood. The hinges repaired themselves, which was much better than just leaning the door against the jamb. "Thank you."

Max turned to find Valeria sitting cross-legged on the center of the floor. A chalk star was etched around her. Wren made a shushing motion.

A moment later, Valeria sagged. "I also found no trace of her."

Unease and fear for Rose twisted his belly. Rose had no magic of her own. That meant someone with magic had stolen her and was hiding her from them. Maybe he'd get lucky and Joshua, Serene, or Master Phil would have a way to find her. He couldn't help feeling like something he had done was what caused Rose to flee.

The door banged open and Joshua, Serene, and Master Phil stormed into the room.

"She's gone. What the hell is going on?" Joshua demanded.

Max fought through his rage. He would do her no good like this. The tingle he'd felt when she passed him meant she was being controlled just like he had been.

"Rose is under someone's control," Valeria said. "I think it's the same person who had control of Max."

Joshua went and took Serene's hand. He made a visible effort to calm down. "Tell me what happened and I'll tell you about what Rose and I discovered."

Serene told them about what they'd discovered with Valeria in the spell circle. Max noticed she didn't mention Max or Rose's relationship or Wren's initial reception.

Joshua wrapped his arm around her and kissed the top of her head. "Did you know Rose was undead too?"

Max's heart stuttered. Rose was undead too?

Serene smiled at Joshua. "It was not my secret to share."

"They are the same kind of undead," Master Phil said. He added a pot to the fire. The contents sloshed as he lifted it. "We can't track her in normal ways. She left behind no scent and is far faster than we are."

"She's also magically blocked from scrying," Wren added.

Max knew from his sister that scrying was a magical distance seeing. Someone had blocked magic to track Rose, which meant they had few clues to find her.

Joshua must have been thinking something similar because he said, "Let me tell you about the cemetery." Joshua told the group about Rose being poisoned by Glenn, the gate, and Calder.

If Rose and Max were undead—and even the same kind—

then maybe the clues in the cemetery could also help Rose. "Did you find anything where Rose and Serene had rescued me?" Max asked.

Joshua shook his head. "The mausoleum had been cleaned out."

"So we're left trying to figure out who is controlling her?" Max asked.

"Or maybe how you got to be as you are," Wren said.

"Max has no knowledge of how he became an undead," Valeria said. "The truth circle would have forced him to reveal it."

Perhaps Max becoming undead was linked to his missing memories, but then how had Rose become one too? "Do you think my memories could be restored?"

"Not by magic." Valeria shook her head. "They'll come back when you're ready."

"Or not at all," Wren added. "What do Max and Rose share?"

"They have being from Hope in common." Serene tried to step away from Joshua.

"Maybe Hope is filled with the living dead. Maybe they were turned when they were protected from the Merge. A spell gone wrong." Joshua pulled her to his chest and nuzzled her ear. Serene's face reddened, and she seemed surprised. Why was Joshua being so overly affectionate to Serene? He glanced at Master Phil, who also seemed puzzled.

"Do undead have children?" Max asked. Hope had been filled with kids and families. Unless everything he had ever known about the living dead was wrong, children were proof the town was living.

"No?" Valeria said, not sounding certain at all.

So, everyone in Hope could be undead. How was this possible? It broke every rule he'd ever heard of regarding the living dead. Perhaps pre-shield movies weren't the most reliable source of information.

"Maybe leaving Hope and crossing the shield is what did it." Wren stared at Joshua, who continued to nuzzle Serene.

"Do we know if anyone else has come across the shield?" Master Phil asked.

"I have no idea." Max said. "No one went near the shield. Warnings were posted. But who knows."

"No kids disappeared?" Master Phil pressed.

"We did have a kid when I was much younger who we know went through the shield. All that was left was his clothing."

"Rose wasn't naked when she came through," Joshua said.

"How could you possibly know that?" Serene scolded. She tried to step away from Joshua.

Joshua pulled her closer. She gave an exasperated eye roll.

Joshua said, "I didn't know it at the time. But I met her right after she crossed over."

"None of this is helping us find her," Max muttered. "It was like she fled."

Suddenly Joshua stood straighter, with arm still tucked around Serene. "Or like she was being called. She said she heard voices. They were calling her to come help them. To save them."

Max swallowed his uneasiness. Rose had been hearing voices as well. "I thought I heard something similar when we were fighting the zombies earlier in Shifterville." Was being undead related to the voices?

"So the zombies and the voices could be related," Serene pushed Joshua's hand away. "Joshua, let go."

"I just want to be near," Joshua said. "I think we need to go back to the cemetery."

"If we find her, what are we going to do? Carry her back?" Max asked. The place she had kicked still throbbed.

"If I have to," Master Phil muttered.

"We need Valeria and Wren to break the spell," Serene said. "They did it once, they can do it again."

"You can use my place if it would help." Master Phil glanced at the door. "I see you fixed the door."

"Sorry. I heard Rose screaming," Max said. He still couldn't believe how easily the door had come off. Whether his strength was due to Rose being in danger or his undead status, he wasn't sure.

"We have another lead," Master Phil said distractedly. He, too, turned to watch Serene slap away Joshua's hands again. Everyone but Valeria watched Joshua's antics with Serene. Max wasn't the only one who found it odd.

Since no one else was saying anything about Joshua and Serene, Max didn't either. "What lead?" Max asked.

"Rose was taking a potion from Glenn from the West District," Joshua said. He didn't seem to notice everyone watching him.

"Why is this a lead?"

"She doesn't remember meeting him," Joshua said. "He knew she was undead and was poisoning her."

"We can take the West Market." Serene pointed at Master Phil.

"It's not safe. I should go with you." Joshua scowled and pulled her closer.

Serene raised her eyebrows at Joshua and sent him a puzzled frown. "You know I'll be fine."

"Wren and I can stay here. We might need to create something more mobile for Rose," Valeria said.

Max needed to check out the cemetery. It seemed there was a good chance Rose was there. Joshua was the only person who had been to the cemetery recently. He'd be able to tell if anything had changed. "Joshua, I think you and I should go to the cemetery," Max said.

Joshua pulled Serene closer and looked about to argue. His jaw was tight and his eyes flashed with anger, but his face had paled and the faint tang of fear invaded the room.

Max stepped back. Why was Joshua acting so oddly? Wren, Serene, and Master Phil had also noticed something was amiss. He didn't know Joshua well, but even to Max his behavior seemed off.

"You see it?" Valeria asked Wren so softly Max barely heard her. He glanced at her and caught her and Wren exchanging a look. They separated and casually moved closer to Joshua.

"What's going on, Lighthouse? You afraid?" Wren asked. His voice was deep and mocking.

Max realized Wren was acting as a distraction. He made big gestures, and his voice was a touch louder than normal. Was Valeria going to hit Joshua with magic?

"What's your problem?" Joshua asked.

"You." Wren stepped closer.

Valeria lunged forward and snagged Joshua's hand. Wren grabbed his other arm, knocking Serene out of the way. Wren wrapped his arms around Joshua from behind. The scent of fear sharpened and hit Max's senses hard.

"Serene." Joshua sounded frantic. He bucked and twisted, but wasn't able to break Wren's hold. "Are you hurt?"

"Open your hand," Valeria demanded.

Joshua's hand was clenched so tightly his fingers were turning white.

Max helped Serene up.

"Let me go! Serene needs me." Joshua's face twisted with fear and rage. His skin was red and his eyes huge and wild.

"Open your hand, and we'll let you go to Serene," Valeria said.

Joshua bucked one last time and then slowly opened his

hand. The necklace Joshua had removed from Rose lay in his palm.

Valeria used a cloth to snatch the broken necklace out of Joshua's grasp.

Joshua's whole body relaxed. He took a shuddery breath. "Thank you. I was deathly afraid of losing Serene."

Max stepped back in shock. Of course! The necklace controlled both Rose and Joshua. Joshua had been frightened of losing Serene, and the fear Rose had toward Hope must have been caused by the necklace. "Why did she run if the necklace was controlling her?"

"I think there may be two different people or factions who have opposite goals involved." Valeria tucked the necklace in her pouch.

"Who?" Max demanded.

Valeria shrugged. "I don't know. We can study the necklace while you find Rose."

Joshua hugged Serene and kissed her soundly. "Stay safe," he whispered to her. "Come on, Max. I need to make a stop before the cemetery."

Joshua led Max down the streets at a fast pace. Max had no time to look around. It wasn't that Joshua was so much faster, it was that he dodged unexpectedly by going between buildings and on top of walls. Max jogged to keep up. He didn't want to get lost in this city.

After more turns than Max could count, Joshua slowed. Max caught sight of a silver box-shaped building with large windows. Above the door hung a sign that said, "Joe's".

"Are we going there?" Max asked.

Joshua nodded and took the lead. He opened the door, which rang a bell. The red-topped booths and black-and-white checkered floor reminded Max of the 50's diners he'd seen in books in Hope.

"Lighthouse. How are you doing?" The large, brown-haired man sat behind the counter.

"I'm good, Joe. I don't have time for food."

Joe was so big he could reach the window to the kitchen. He grabbed two brown paper bags. "There's always time for food." Joe handed both Joshua and Max each a bag. The aroma of fries and a burger wafted from it. Max's stomach growled at the smell. How did Joe know they were coming?

Max took out one of the fries and bit into it. The fry was just the way he liked his fries, crisp and hot.

"Thanks Joe." Joshua leaned closer and his face lost all trace of humor. "Rose is in trouble."

Joe stopped smiling. "Tell me more."

"She's under a spell. She's untraceable, and we have no idea where she is."

"Does it have anything to do with the zombies wandering through the city?" Joe asked. Did his question mean Joe knew Rose was undead?

"It might," Joshua said.

Joe nodded. "I'll see what's on the network. Put the word out to find her."

Max thought back to the wallop she'd given him. He didn't want anyone getting hurt. "Don't approach. She's not herself."

Joe nodded.

"Thanks Joe," Joshua said.

They walked out, and the bell jingled behind them.

Joshua tore open his bag as if he had been holding himself back from eating. He crunched on a fry. "Joe is good people and makes the best damn burger and fries."

Max knew that wasn't all that had happened. "And?"

"And happens to be in the center of the best information network in the whole city. Joe knew we were heading his way and with enough time for him to get the burgers ready."

"And fries." Max popped another fry in his mouth. He hadn't realized how hungry he was until he'd smelled them. "Does he give everyone burgers?"

Joshua took out his burger and took a bite. "Reminds me of when I was a kid."

"Yeah, me too," Max said, feeling a strange kinship with Joshua.

Joshua grinned. "That's why we got burgers."

Max stopped walking and wondered what that implied about Joe and his network.

"Come on." Joshua led them across a bridge and through a maze of buildings. They soon came upon a gate with a strange mist floating around it.

The hairs on Max's back rose with dread. He knew it was a cemetery. He sniffed the air and expected the same smell of earth and rot he'd scented with the zombies, but didn't smell anything. His skin prickled with magic nearby. On top of the sense of magic was like an electric edge that felt sinister. He had the odd sense the fence had been made to keep him out and would hurt him if he came in contact with the bars. "I really do not want to touch those bars," Max said.

"Damn, I'd forgotten about that." Joshua glanced around. "If I put up a ladder, are you willing to crawl over?"

Max didn't want to touch the fence, but he certainly had to get over it to have a chance at helping Rose. "That's better."

Joshua came back with a ladder and leaned it against the gate. Max couldn't believe he was about to break into a cemetery in the middle of the city.

He'd expected something nice on a hill away from the city. The Hope cemetery had been almost to the shield on the East side. The gate around it had been more ornamental than to keep people out. This gate was designed to keep people out. Or in.

Joshua went up first and dropped over the edge. Max

climbed the ladder until he was almost to the top. The next rung was where the ladder leaned on the fence. He'd have to touch it. The thought made his skin crawl, but for Rose he would do it.

He grabbed a tree limb by his head for support and stood on the last rung. He took a breath and then stepped onto the fence top. He could feel the malevolent magic through his shoes. He dropped lightly on the other side.

Max scented the air. Some mold and decay came through. He could smell the sweat from Joshua, and the trees and grass, but no undead.

Joshua walked forward scanning. "Still quiet."

"What now?" The huge cemetery was far bigger than he had expected. If his hunch was right and Rose was here, they'd have a hard time finding her.

"Can you hear the voices too?" Joshua asked while scanning the area.

Max held his breath and listened. He heard the scratch of branches rubbing together. A cat, probably outside the fence, yowled. Disappointment stabbed his chest. "I hear nothing."

Joshua closed his eyes and his brow furrowed. Max stood still. The fine hairs on the back of his neck rose. It was almost as if Joshua was looking around without moving.

A flash of motion low to the ground caught his eye. He followed past the brush and saw a rat hop across one of a dozen headstones. In front of the stones, the graves were sunken in, as if the people inside had climbed out. Max shouldn't be shocked at empty graves. He knew the undead here were restless. He just hadn't expected to see the evidence so clearly. He went back to Joshua.

After a moment more, Joshua sagged. "Nothing. I found nothing."

"You found no sign of Rose?" Max stepped closer. Joshua might need help. Whatever he had done had made him tired.

"Yes, and no sign of any undead."

Were the undead here suddenly not restless any longer? What about the empty graves he had just seen? "What does that mean?"

"That we have thousands of missing undead."

15

———

ROSE

Early evening, Primum second, 295 years post-Merge

R ose felt as if she were surrounded by a thousand people, but no one was there. She couldn't quite open her eyes. Should that worry her? Her thoughts were muted.

Since she couldn't move, she drifted back to her last days in Hope, five years before. There was a puzzle there that worried her. It had started with Mistress Yaneli's summons.

Rose had crumpled the invitation in her hand. And took a deep breath. She didn't want to be away from her children for even a moment, but when Mistress Yaneli called, she had to go.

She peeked into the bedroom. Her girls were sleeping in the same bed. She didn't want to leave them. They both wore black shirts in mourning. Regret and sadness filtered into her body, and she closed her eyes. She missed him. Maybe Mistress Yaneli was going to give her condolences on the loss of her husband.

Rose laughed at her own nonsense. Mistress Yaneli had

never shown any interest in Rose, since she wasn't one of the magical people in the town. As far as Rose knew, she had no magical abilities whatsoever. That turned out to be a blessing in a way, because it left her a lot of free time. While the other kids went to required magic training, she'd sparred.

So, to be called by Mistress Yaneli was rare enough under most circumstances, but because of how things had been the last few months, odd was scary. She shook off the feeling.

If she were going to go to Mistress Yaneli's, this was the best time. The kids had just fallen asleep. The next-door neighbor was in the house to help Rose and would take care of the kids.

Rose could say no. She had the excuse of her husband's funeral being yesterday. Anyone else in town would understand but not Mistress Yaneli. What she commanded, the town did. It wasn't that she got angry, but more that bad things happened to those who didn't follow her wishes. The thought was unsettling.

She sighed. She'd have to go.

The note to the neighbor only took her a moment to write. She slipped out the front door and headed down the lane. She was at the one edge of town where the houses were smaller. The cluck of chickens and the bark of a dog seemed muted in the morning.

Mistress Yaneli's house was the largest and sat in the center of town. She'd owned it for as long as Rose could remember. Rose had never been inside. It was a large Victorian house with a gate and a garden. She'd heard there were rooms downstairs where the apprentices would work and practice. The next level held more advanced students. Only the best of the best were able to get into her house.

The top room was where Mistress Yaneli lived. Rose didn't know anyone who had been to the top. Would she get a chance to see that floor?

No one else was out yet on errands. The orderly blocks were

empty. Picture books showed cars, but they'd never made any sense to her. Not when she could walk from one end of town to the other in an hour.

The grass was brown and dried. If she were to look at their gardens, she would probably see the same thing she saw in her own. Dried and dying plants, which were struggling to live. Dying, like the people in town.

She thought again of her two girls. They both had brown curly. They both had her sense of humor but their daddy's face. Both of them looked so much like their daddy that her heart clenched when they turned to her. He was the most recent to die. She worried who would be next.

"Are you sure you should do this?" Eleanor, Rose's best friend and sister-in-law walked up. She seemed paler than normal. Her eyes, usually so full of mischief, were dull. Her mouth pulled down in a frown.

Rose jumped. "You startled me." She hadn't heard Eleanor. Rose knew Eleanor grieved for her brother just as Rose did. "Are you sure you should be out?"

Eleanor gave a grim smile. "I'm your wing-woman."

"You're sweet. What do I have to fear from Mistress Yaneli?"

Eleanor looked at her for a long moment and then looked away. "There are some who whisper that she is the reason we are all sick." Her voice was barely above a whisper.

"Why would she do that?" Rose had also heard the rumors and had dismissed them. Mistress Yaneli had apprentices and high level people who had also succumbed to the sickness. Did someone have to die to prove they were not at fault?

So silly.

Eleanor shook her head, seemingly not willing to speculate on Mistress Yaneli. Rose knew her friend was worried about Rose.

"I'll be fine alone. I swear," Rose said. She would see what

Mistress Yaneli wanted and go back to her kids. The sooner she went the sooner she could be home.

"Did you know Max was called as well? Doesn't that strike you as suspicious?" Eleanor walked next to her, keeping pace, but the long sentence seemed to drain her.

Rose tilted her head. It was odd that both she and Max would be summoned. His ties with her husband and Eleanor had made him a close friend. They were two of only a few people with no magic. "No."

"Seriously?" Eleanor's face became a little more animated. A flush spread across her cheeks.

Rose purposely quirked her eyebrows at Eleanor. "This is not another of your doomsday prophecies?"

Eleanor stiffened and assumed a formal posture with her shoulders thrown back and her chin lifted. "I do have a little bit of premonition in my blood."

Rose grinned at Eleanor's deft mimicry of Mistress Yaneli's apprentices. The whole stance was made even funnier by Eleanor's tiny stature. She was a full head shorter than Rose.

Eleanor slouched. "You might not believe me, but I know for a fact that you and Max are linked somehow and there are bad times ahead." Eleanor rubbed her forehead.

Rose saw the sweat run down her neck.

Eleanor frowned. "Just please be careful."

"Aren't I always?"

Eleanor snorted a laugh. "Really? You were more trouble than all the rest of the kids in our class."

Rose shared the smile. Eleanor was right. It was only when Rose found martial arts that she'd been able to tame the restless energy she had inside of her. Her martial arts skill made her feel less like an outcast when she was able to do something so phys-ical that few bothered with. "I'll be careful."

Eleanor frowned and stuffed her hands in her pockets. The

soft sound of her panting seemed loud in the night air. Something was wrong. Rose spun to look at her friend.

Eleanor tried to smile, but it came out as a grimace. There was sweat on her upper lip. Her eyes seemed to unfocus as Rose watched. Something was very wrong.

Eleanor swayed. "I'm glad you are my friend."

Rose touched Eleanor's cheek. Heat burned beneath her fingertips, and Rose's heart thundered in her chest. No. No, Eleanor couldn't be sick.

Eleanor's eyes rolled back. Rose caught her before she fell.

Panic clogged her veins. She lifted Eleanor up, shocked at how little she weighed. Her stomach twisted.

Rose turned her back on Mistress Yaneli's house. She had to do everything she could to save her friend.

16

MAX

Early evening, Primum second, 300 years post-Merge

The wind howled through the fence around the cemetery, sending an icy chill down Max's back. He gazed around to his right at the leaning gravestones next to Joshua. Did they lean because the undead had risen and left the area? Thousands of missing undead seemed crazy.

Joshua's expression didn't look as if he were kidding.

"But Rose could still be here," Max said. Even as the words left his lips he knew Rose wasn't in the cemetery.

Joshua shook his head. "Unless she is hidden by some very powerful magic, Rose is not within the cemetery."

Max wondered how Joshua knew, and at the same time believed him.

"Where do we try next?" Max knew nothing about the town. He wasn't even sure where Rose lived.

A crunch of a foot on a gravel path sounded off to his left, toward the direction of the main gate. A tall man with a hawk nose separated from the shadows and headed straight for Joshua.

"Oh, thank goddess." He stopped within a few feet of Joshua. He ran his hand through his hair. His eyes were wide and worried. "We have a problem."

"Calder. Tell me more." Joshua sounded controlled and almost bored. Had Joshua said Calder's name so Max would know he was the undead expert?

Max worked to mirror Joshua's stance. He didn't want to ruin anything Joshua might be doing. The fact that an undead expert was worried made what Joshua had said earlier more believable.

"All the dead are gone." Calder made a wide gesture with his hands, which seemed to encompass the whole cemetery.

So, the undead didn't just wander away? The way Calder was acting seemed to say no.

"Any idea where they went?" Joshua came across like he didn't care, but something about the way his stance shifted, and the way he held his shoulders made Max think Joshua was worried. Perhaps Joshua was using the bored tone to get more information?

"No, you don't understand." Calder wrung his hands and then ran his hands through his hair again. "They didn't wander away. They were taken."

Joshua whistled long and low. Joshua didn't believe Calder and wanted him to know that. "What makes you think they were taken?"

"I checked the graves. They're all empty." Calder's face went red and his eyes widened, which made him look embarrassed and outraged at the same time.

"That doesn't mean someone took them," Joshua said.

Max flicked his gaze between the two men. Calder was the picture of befuddled outrage. The look was made complete by a spark of anger in his gaze. Joshua was cool and bored and continued to watch Calder.

Max did think the undead were gone. He didn't scent anything in the cemetery. The stillness around them wasn't natural. He'd been so sure Rose would be here. He couldn't explain why, but he felt like she had been. Which meant that maybe whoever took the undead had taken Rose as well.

"I put up a magical aura that made the undead not see the townsfolk nearby." Calder let out a breath and clenched his hands into fists. "What I was doing should have contained them. They would have no reason to leave the cemetery. Someone had to have been siphoning the undead away. I was a fool."

Max opened up his new senses again. There was a stillness to the air. He didn't have a particular pull any longer. Nothing called to him. The voices were completely gone.

"Who could do that?" Joshua asked.

"I'm not sure." Calder put his hands on his hips and stared at Joshua. "You have to help me get them back where they belong. The dead are meant to be at peace."

Even though his face hadn't changed, something about Joshua's eyes showed his interest.

"Anyone new or odd near the cemetery?" Joshua asked.

"It's so big, and there are four entrances. I would have no way of knowing if someone jumped the fence." Calder looked like he might say something else, but stopped.

Max waited to see what Calder would say. The silence felt like a heavy brooding thing that sat on his chest. He wanted to scream. They needed to find Rose before something terrible happened to her. What was Joshua waiting for?

Then Calder snapped his fingers. "You know, a couple months ago I was here, and so was a man who seemed too interested in the cemetery. He was acting oddly. What was his name?"

He closed his eyes, pressing his fingertips to his temples. "Ben? Garry? No, it was Glenn."

Joshua's gaze met Max's. Glenn was on their list. They already knew he had tried to poison Rose with a potion, and he knew she was undead. But why would he take all the undead when he'd been trying to kill Rose?

"What did he say he wanted to do with the dead?" Joshua asked. "Hating or destroying undead isn't a crime."

The only laws Max had ever heard about the dead was not to take their stuff because of curses. And that only seemed to apply to mummies from before the shield.

"He said he'd raise his own undead army if he had to," Calder said.

The word 'army' brought Max up short. Joshua stood straighter.

"Could he do that?" Max asked.

Calder shrugged. "He stormed away soon after."

"Did he say anything else?" Joshua asked.

"Something about 'Stregs.'" Calder looked confused. "I have only heard that term with trolls. But he seemed to imply humans."

"Damn it." Joshua muttered under his breath. He looked away as if debating what to do.

Max wanted to ask Joshua more questions, but he didn't want to in front of Calder. Even if the city council had sent him, Joshua didn't seem to trust the man.

Max had heard enough to know something big happened recently. Joshua and Serene had been in the middle of saving the world. Rose and Serene had found Max when searching for the culprits. And the plot against the world, too, had to do with undead.

"Does that mean something to you?" Calder tugged on Joshua's arm.

Joshua stepped out of his reach. "Someone figured out how to use the troll disease to infect humans and magically enhance the humans to control the rage that sickness produced. The 'Streg' almost overran the city."

Calder's mouth opened wide and then snapped shut. His gaze flicked to Joshua and then away.

Max wondered what someone would use an undead army for. He pictured the zombies they had run into and creating an army of zombies seemed pointless. The zombies had been easily distracted. A good army should be coordinated and purposeful. Then he remembered what he'd been told about a horde. "Do you think he's trying to create a horde?"

Both Joshua and Calder jerked to look at him. They both had the same shocked but penetrating stare.

"Maybe. I'm not sure how he would control a horde," Calder said slowly. "There are ways to magically bind them to do a mage's bidding. But it's very intensive. It would take a very powerful mage to do it."

The wizards in Hope were always looking for ways to make spells simpler. The act of casting was already arduous, so any extra effort increased the odds the spell would fail.

"You had mentioned an intelligent undead might be able to," Joshua said.

Cold flickered through Max. An image of an open grave and an undead being drawn out filled his mind. Was the image from his past?

"Theoretically," Calder said. "It would still take a powerful mage."

"So it hasn't happened before?" Joshua asked.

"No, it would also take a very special, very intelligent undead. Someone trained to control their body. The undead would act as an extension," Calder said.

Just like Rose. She'd be perfect for the job of controlling an undead army. The martial arts training she had gave her great body coordination. Max, on the other hand, wouldn't be great. He'd done more bookish things in his life and did trip over his own feet occasionally.

"We need more information." Joshua strode toward the front gate.

"Thanks for your help," Max said and hurried to follow Joshua.

Calder ran to block them and held out his hands in a stop gesture. "I'm coming with you."

Max jerked back. Did he want an undead expert with them now that Max knew he, too, was undead?

"I can't bring you," Joshua said. "It's too dangerous."

"I know I made a mistake, but I want to make amends."

Joshua shook his head and walked around Calder.

"Please. The people trusted me. I have to help fix the mess I made." He ran back in front of Joshua and looked at both Max and Joshua with appeal in his eyes. "Please."

Calder looked so sincere and truly seemed to want to help. Maybe Calder posed no risk to Max, but would he be able to help them locate the undead or assist in determining what was making the dead so restless?

Joshua hesitated. "Damn it," Joshua said with a sigh under his breath.

"Bring him. You never know when having an undead expert would come in handy," Max said.

"Fine," Joshua said. "Let's get to Master Phil's."

Calder led them out of the cemetery. He paused at the gate and locked it when they passed.

The way Calder moved seemed very familiar to Max. He had a slight limp on his right side. "Have we met before?" Max finally asked.

"No, I don't think so."

"You remind me of someone," Max said. The feeling that this was somehow important persisted. Could this man be a part of his missing memories?

Calder grinned at Max. "I'm sure there's at least one other person who looks like me." He chuckled, but didn't share the joke.

Max nodded, but couldn't shake the feeling they had met before.

It didn't take long to cross the city. The sun was setting and as the shadows lengthened, the feeling of the air changed.

Max could smell more creatures coming to life. That meant Rose was alone in the night. His stomach twisted. He lost track of the turns they took through the city, but he was sure it hadn't taken this long to get to the cemetery. Had Joshua gone a longer way to get to Master Phil's? Did Joshua not trust Calder because he trusted so few?

Joshua knocked in a coded way on the door Max had ripped off. The hinge still looked odd, but the door swung open smoothly.

Master Phil was at the door, peering behind them. His expression was hopeful. "Did you find her?"

"No." Joshua stepped in. "Where's Serene?"

"She had another idea—" Master Phil eyed Calder. The look wasn't hostile, but it wasn't friendly either. "Who's this?"

"Calder. He's an undead expert," Joshua said.

Respect for Joshua increased. He let Master Phil know this was the person Rose and he had met at the cemetery without Calder knowing.

Master Phil nodded and stepped back. "Come in."

Max followed Joshua into Master Phil's home. The curtain was still up, but Wren and Valeria were nowhere to be seen. They must have just left, because he scented them heavily in the room. Had they been able to figure out a spell to save Rose?

"Hungry?" Master Phil asked.

"A little." Joshua glanced at Max and gave him a small smile. Max was sure Joshua was just as full as he was on burgers and fries.

"Sit here." Master Phil pointed at a chair.

Calder sat at the table while Master Phil set it. "What happened?"

"We discovered that the cemetery had been emptied of undead," Joshua said.

Master Phil paused in reaching for a cup. "Why would someone do that?"

"We think they might be forming an army," Max said. That conclusion felt correct. Why was a whole different question. He hadn't seen anything here so far to indicate the people in this town were oppressed. The market he had seen had been full, and the people seemed to get along fine. "But why?"

"They could have a grudge against specific people." Joshua glanced at Master Phil and something exchanged between them.

"Use the army on the city itself," Master Phil stated.

"Or the neighboring city," Joshua added.

"That's scary. So, we really have no idea." Max sat and pulled his chair in to get out of Master Phil's way. The space seemed crowded with so many people at the table.

"The HPA network is down, so I have no idea what the rumors are in town. I reached out to Joe to see what he could find." Joshua sat next to Max.

"Good idea. I could see what the Shifters have to say. As of yesterday, all they were talking about were the lights in the sky from the UnMerge attempt. There have been a few Streg sightings. But nothing else has caught anyone's attention." Master Phil took out bowls and ladled from the pot on the fire.

He handed them each a container of stew. Joshua's and Max's weren't as full as Calder's bowl.

Max picked at his food and watched Joshua and Calder. An undead army that could be used to attack anything was a hard lead to follow. "It could be something else entirely. A deeper game we don't know about," Max said.

Joshua nodded. "Someone has to know the players. It's hard to keep stuff like that secret."

"What would it take to steal the undead from the cemetery?" Max turned and looked at Calder.

Calder blew on a spoonful of stew. "You could have a team. One person would be the bait, lead them out, and then put them in a special cage. Any life force nearby would distract them. So, it would be very dangerous."

"Your sigils on the windows helped keep the undead from being distracted," Joshua said.

Calder sighed and put his spoon down. "I was so focused on trying to keep the people safe, it never even occurred to me I might be manipulated."

Max's throat ached in sympathy. It wasn't always easy to do the right thing. The bad people in the world made it even harder.

"It happens to the best of us," Joshua said, looking sympathetic. "So you get these undead out of the cemetery and magically drawn somewhere, and you set up stuff to block out distractions. Then what? They haven't attacked. What are they waiting for?"

"They must be contained," Calder said.

"I know undead can be dangerous, but why would they need to be contained?" Joshua asked.

"If the person was trying to make a horde, the undead would have to be kept closely together while the magic was cast," Calder said.

Did that mean Rose might be caged up somewhere with the zombies? He shuddered.

"Could they all be put in the same cage?" Joshua asked.

Calder shook his head. "They're a bit like magnets that way."

"How so?" Joshua paused with the spoon part way to his mouth. A strange expression crossed his face, but he cleared it quickly and took a bite. Had Calder said something odd?

"Magnets can repel other magnets," Calder said.

"Or attract them." Max thought of the magnets he had played with as a kid in Hope.

"That's true. They could only be built a certain way before the walls collapse," Calder said.

"What would that look like dealing with undead?" Joshua asked.

"The undead will turn on each other if you try to put too many in the same place," Calder said.

"So they would destroy each other?" Joshua asked.

Calder nodded. "It would be better if they didn't notice each other."

The door banged open. Serene rushed in. "I know how to find him."

"Who?" Joshua pushed his bowl away and stood.

"Glenn," Serene said.

17

———

ROSE

Early evening, Primum second, 295 years post-Merge

"Go to sleep," commanded a voice Rose thought she recognized.

Her mind drifted back to Hope and the puzzle from five years ago.

Rose pressed her forehead against the cool wood of the door of Eleanor's house. Her hands clenched. She wanted to be inside with her friend, but the doctor asked her to wait outside.

Max was inside with his wife. Rose longed to comfort him. The thought of her friend dying and Max being alone clenched her hands and poured acid in her gut.

The door opened, and she stepped back. She blinked her eyes against the forming tears. Max shook the doctor's hand.

"Remember what I told you," the doctor said.

Max nodded, and the doctor walked away.

Max's face was pinched and the dark circles under his eyes were even deeper. "Come in." He sounded exhausted.

The door clicked behind her.

"Eleanor's not doing well." His gaze traveled down the hall and further into the back of the house. "Doctor says she will die later today."

Rose sagged against the door frame. Tears came heavier in her eyes. "I'm not sure I can take her dying too." Rose's kids were with the neighbor, and they weren't doing well either. Would anything go right?

Max nodded and opened his arms for a hug.

She hugged him. "I'm so sorry. I love her too."

Max shook. "Mistress Yaneli summoned me. I just—"

A sharp rap at the door interrupted what else he might have said.

Rose gave Max one last squeeze and opened the door to see a tattered-looking young man. Ferrik was one of the better known of Mistress Yaneli's apprentices.

His wizard robes shimmered in the sunlight. "Rose, she really needs to see you."

Rose couldn't keep Mistress Yaneli at bay any longer. Rose touched Max's shoulder. "I'll stop by later."

Max nodded.

Rose followed Ferrik down the block. She felt so bad leaving her two friends. She glanced back, expecting to see the door closed, but Max stood on the porch. He stared after her, looking lost and forlorn. It left her stomach tied in knots. Someone needed to stop the plague before more good people died.

She cleared her throat and turned back to Ferrik. "Do you have any idea what Mistress Yaneli wants to see me about?"

Ferrik glanced at her and shook his head. "No, she's been locked up in her tower." He must have seen her confusion because he added, "That's what we call her room. She's been in there for too long."

"Why does she want to see me?" Mistress Yaneli was being

insistent. Rose's stomach twisted. Why her? Surely one of the magically talented people in Hope was a better choice for whatever Mistress Yaneli wanted. It wasn't like she even had any medical or healing knowledge Mistress Yaneli might need.

"When the first person fell sick, I overheard Mistress Yaneli say she had to fix things." Ferrik dodged her question while he swung his arms and stretched his legs. He seemed to be glad to be outside.

"What do you know about what's going on?" she asked. The odds that Ferrik would say anything were low. The apprentices in Mistress Yaneli's house tended to isolate. Even if he told her nothing, just asking might distract her from Max and her sick friend and sick children.

"Not much. If you learn anything when you see her, let me know."

She hoped this interview would be quick. She needed to check on her kids and on Eleanor. Maybe she could bring some food for Max. He was looking thinner than she liked. She could use a good distraction. "What do you do all day?"

He shrugged. "We study."

She smiled in encouragement and hoped he would keep talking.

"We each have a topic that we study. There are books and such to look at, but we also experiment."

"On what?"

"How things work. Mostly we try to figure out how to remove the shield."

"Why take down the shield?" She stopped and fear shifted from her neck to the small of the back. She'd grown up thinking the shield was the best thing ever. It protected them from the evils of the outside world. The fact that the mistress of the town wanted it down seemed crazy.

He glanced at her and grinned. "This is the first time there have been so many wizards in a small location."

She sighed. He was going to lead her to the answer, instead of just telling her the answer. He wouldn't continue otherwise. She asked the obvious question. "Why does this town have so many?"

"This town was founded by two brothers who married two sisters. They wanted a place that would allow them to be wizards without the normals interfering."

"They established Hope." She did know about the founding brothers and sisters.

"Yes. And when the great shielding happened, and we were shut off from the outside world... Well, the occurrence of whatever genes make us wizards became concentrated."

"What happened to the outside world?"

"No one knows." He raised his brow and paused, seeming to see if she had any other irrelevant questions. "Calder had a premonition just before the event and created the shield to protect us." He started puffing as he walked up the little hill that led to Town Square.

The green space in the middle of Town Square once had two striking oaks with three statues in the middle. The oaks' leaves now hung limp and the once-green grass lay parched. The sting of tears pressed against her eyes. This had been so beautiful. Just as the town had been, but now so many people were dead.

A white marble bench stood so one could gaze upon the statues. Ferrik made his way to the bench and sat down. She paused in surprise. Weren't they supposed to be hurrying to Mistress Yaneli?

He took a few deep breaths and pulled out a cloth to blot his face. The pulse on his neck thumped wildly. He was just like the town. Weak from suffering.

Normally the area would have held people going on errands

or just talking in the town center. But since the sickness first started, people tended to isolate themselves in their houses. She missed the people. Especially the kids.

A bird fluttered to land on one of the statues. She and Ferrik were alone.

Rose stared at the statues to give Ferrik a moment to catch his breath.

The first two statues stood near each other. The man stood protectively by the woman. The woman had her chin tilted up stubbornly with her hands on her waist, and gave the impression she could move mountains with her determination. The bronze didn't allow any color, but she had long hair twisted up in a knot at the back of her head. The town needed that sort of determination now.

The man stood behind her, almost touching the woman. His legs were braced apart with his arms and his hands out as if he were holding something back. He had thick brows and the hawkish nose so common in the town. Another man stood back to back with him . Almost as if they were in combat and defending each other's back.

Because the vegetation was failing, she was able to see more detail on the statues. She might even be able to get close to inspect them.

She glanced at her companion. He seemed to need another minute to catch his breath, and she gave into her curiosity.

The other man had the same hawkish nose and stood in a similar stance to the first man. The statue must be to scale because standing next to it made her feel like the man could be right next to her. He'd be a few inches taller than her. His hair looked wild, as if he were always running his hand through it. He wore a necklace, which was common enough with mages.

Rose stepped closer to look at the necklace and stumbled on bits of bronze on the ground in front of him. She parted the crackling grass. Two dainty bronze feet still stood on the spot. The rest of the figure had been broken off at the ankles. Scrolled on a nameplate between the two feet was the word 'Ember.' Rose recognized her name as one of the founding sisters.

"If there were four of them, why not show all four?" she asked Ferrik, who had finally joined her in front of the statues.

Ferrik glanced around. He scooted forward and stood next to her near the statues. "We think there had been another figure, but it was torn down." His voice was just over a whisper.

"Why would someone tear down a statue of one of our founders?" She used the same volume as he had. She wasn't sure why that was a secret. "It would be one of the sisters who was missing. Right?"

Ferrik nodded. "It was destroyed hundreds of years ago. The reason has been lost through time." He was still whispering.

"Why are we whispering?"

Something flashed across his face as he glanced at her.

His gaze made her nervous. Then he started walking again. Was he avoiding talking about the missing woman, or had he suddenly realized how slow he had been to retrieve her?

This was the fastest she had seen him walk. As if he couldn't wait to get away from the statues. As if something about even knowing the existence of them was dangerous.

She caught up with him easily. His lips were pressed in a firm line, and he wouldn't look at her. Perhaps he was angry. She sighed. Mages were always in a huff over something.

He marched up the stairs to the huge Victorian house. His hands shook so hard, he couldn't quite open the door. His hands shook too hard.

He wasn't angry, he was scared. What could he be scared of?

Eleanor's words from earlier whispered at her. What if there was more going on with Mistress Yaneli? A chill went up Rose's back.

The door opened with a creak, and he ushered her inside. The room had probably once been a grand entrance, but now the floor was brown and warped. Water dripped down the wall to her right. The once-fine wallpaper bulged. Was the house affected by the plague somehow? She knew the house was odd, even for a mage's house.

She stepped in. A crystal chandelier jangled with each step, and dust snowed down as it quaked. The dust dulled the glass of the chandelier hung on a grayed ceiling. A broad stairway led up. A mouse scurried past and went into a hole next to a closed door. A shiver again ran down her spine. The whole place felt creepy and off. She'd expected something luxuriant and well-kept.

Ferrik led her up the stairs to the second floor. The last stair creaked as she stepped on it. The smell of must and decay was more prominent on this level. She glanced at Ferrik, whose face was set in a grim line. He looked tormented. There was no hopeful glimmer, just resignation. Pity stirred her heart. It must be horrible living in such a place.

"What happened?" She asked softly. The outside of the house looked fine, but the inside seemed to be from a much older house that hadn't been maintained.

His gaze darted to her. He must have seen the sympathy on her face because he started talking in a low, rushed voice. "A few years ago I found her on the floor. Unconscious." His lips pressed together. "I thought she was dead."

Unease sent more shivers down her spine. The sickness started a few years ago. Could the Mistress's bout of unconsciousness be linked to the sickness?

"She woke up a few moments later, looking red-eyed and haggard. She said damn him for blocking the channel." Ferrik's gaze jerked to Rose.

Rose remembered a school acquaintance who had a magical

connection with another. They'd called it a soul-bond. Said it happened to mated mages. They could talk even if they were nowhere near each other. Could that be the magical channel?

Rose waited for more. He seemed caught in the memory, as if it haunted him. She waited, unsure if she should touch him or offer sympathy.

"Everything changed after that." His gaze focused on her face. An unexpected mix of pleading and shame crossed his features. The things I've—"

"Is she here?" A cultured female voice floated down from the next level.

The coldness of the voice caused Rose to step back. That voice didn't sound like the voice of a town savior. It sounded more like the bad guy in the old movies they'd watched before the plague.

"Yes, Mistress Yaneli." Ferrik's voice sounded calm, detached, and so different from the wild emotions that had played across his expressions moments earlier.

"Send her up," Mistress Yaneli said.

"Yes, ma'am." And then he leaned in and whispered in her ear so that she could barely hear him, "I'm sorry. I'll do what I can."

He made a motion at the bottom of the stairs. Something shimmered, and it was as if a curtain parted. The next floor lightened. He wouldn't look at her, and a trace of tears ran down his averted face.

Confusion warred within her. This wasn't at all what she'd been expecting. She had always heard what a privilege it was to be chosen to be in this house. The plague and the famine must be taking its toll here as well. She hadn't expected the smell of decay or Mistress Yaneli's cold voice.

The plague didn't explain the fear she had seen on Ferrik's face. Nor did it explain the inside of this house or Ferrik's apology. What did he have to apologize for? She resisted the urge to ask him. She understood he was being watched. It could be dangerous for him.

Rose took a deep breath. There probably wasn't much the Mistress Yaneli could do with Rose since she hadn't a speck of natural magical abilities. Hopefully, the interview would be quick, and she could get back to her kids, Eleanor, and Max. The people who really needed her.

She fought down the uneasy feeling that once she went up these stairs everything would change.

18

MAX

<u>Early evening, Primum second, 300 years post-Merge</u>

Max ran after Serene. The thought of finding the man who was poisoning Rose put an extra lift in his step.

He focused on breathing and keeping up with Serene's retreating form. She was worse than Joshua with how quickly she traversed the town now. Perhaps she felt the same way he did about finding Rose.

He bumped into a woman carrying a bag, and she dropped it. "Sorry." He grabbed the bag quickly and handed it back to her. He couldn't do more, or he'd lose Serene.

The crazy houses flew by too fast for him to know if he'd been here before. The cobbled and then dirt streets didn't seem familiar.

Ahead, the houses gave way to a rolling field. Vegetable gardens and grains were laid out in patterns on the hillside, which made the planting areas look like a quilt. A path cut between the fields and led to a forest.

As he got closer, he saw that the trees were bigger than anything he had seen in person. They looked like the giant sequoia in the picture books. Twenty people could link hands and still not be able to go all the way around the trunks. The smell of pine and woody growth swamped him.

Serene stopped where the path entered the forest. She wasn't even out of breath after the mad dash across town. Then he realized he wasn't either. Just like his newfound strength, this endurance must come from being undead.

A crack behind him had him turning. Joshua and Calder staggered up, and both were out of breath. Joshua grinned at Serene who winked back.

"The shop was empty, but I got the idea to cross-scent the bottle with the shop. There was a human's scent in both places. It was very faint," Serene said.

"The staff knew nothing," Master Phil added. "I couldn't think of a way to follow a trail that old and stale through the city."

"I wondered if he went outside of the city? And then decided the best place to start was by the Great Preserve," Serene added.

"Why there?" Joshua asked.

"That's where all the crazy secrets are," she stated, and then grinned at Joshua.

Max didn't get the joke.

"Did you find something?" Calder asked sharply.

Serene narrowed her eyes. "Who's this?"

"Calder is an undead expert. The city council had sent him to deal with the zombies," Max said.

Serene raised her eyebrows, but after glancing at Joshua, her gaze returned to Calder. "Yes, I picked up the trail."

Master Phil stepped toward her and sniffed the air. "I think we are going to need our furry forms for this next part."

"Why's that?" Max asked.

Master Phil shrugged. "Better sense of smell and lower to the ground."

Master Phil stripped and put his clothing in a pack. His body rippled, his hair grew, and he hunched forward. His body shifted until he was smaller with dark fur. Another slightly smaller wolf nudged the first. Max goggled; the second time seeing Master Phil transform was just as wondrous.

The two wolves wiggled into wolf-sized backpacks, put their noses to the ground, and headed toward the path going in.

If Calder wasn't here, he might have put his nose to the ground as well, but Max didn't want Calder knowing he was undead.

Instead, he breathed in the air at his level, trying to sort through the scents. He seemed to have abilities now in line with what the Shifters could do. He took in a breath of air. The ground would get him better data, but he still got some scents. A garbled mess of hundreds, if not thousands, of scents came in on that single breath.

Serene and Master Phil entered the forest. The wolves ahead made no sound as they followed the trail only they could sense.

Max followed, stepping carefully on the path just wider than his foot. His footfalls crunched, sounding loud compared to the faint calls of birds, or maybe they were bugs in the distance.

Plants seemed to pat his legs with soft, curious fingers, which sent a shiver down his spine. His imagination was running away with him. Plants weren't curious. But he couldn't shake the feeling something was watching him.

The wind whispered, bringing a hint of the scents from his right. Again, he wished he could get closer to the ground.

Calder stepped on something that snapped a few feet

behind him. He frowned at the ground or possibly at his own feet. He glanced up and caught Max gazing at him. He looked confused. "What is she following?" Calder asked.

"Her nose." There were so many other smells in the Preserve, and Max wasn't sure what they were. He relaxed and took in more air. He picked apart the layers of scent; it was like eating a great soup that had good flavor.

There was the underlying tree smell. Each tree was like passing a person who stood still, but there was an undercurrent of communication he could almost understand.

Then there were the fast-moving animals. The squirrels, the birds, the chipmunks, and snakes. They flitted across his senses leaving a momentary impression of activity.

Then there were the slower moving animals. The skunks, foxes, and cats seemed to go from hiding spot to hiding spot, leaving more aroma behind than their faster and smaller moving counterparts.

There were scents in each category he didn't understand. They must be creatures of myth that lived in the forest.

None of those seemed to be what Serene was following.

Once he separated out those smells he realized there was another layer under that. A trail ahead smelled faintly like mint and even more faintly as human male. That could be the smell Serene followed.

If it was, then many of the other creatures also interacted with the scent. Or at least had stood at almost the same place at the same time. He must not be interpreting the fragrance correctly. He made a note to ask Master Phil.

"Do you have any idea who Glenn is?" Max asked Calder.

A flash of something nasty crossed his expression that Max was unable to interpret. "I'm not sure."

Calder was lying.

"Have you ever seen him before?" Max asked. He wondered if he pushed, would Calder admit to knowing Glenn?

Calder sighed and rubbed his eyes. "The only time I've seen *Glenn* is at the cemetery."

More lies.

Max waited, trying to use what Joshua had done earlier.

"I need to water a tree," Calder said, and then went back the way they had come.

It was funny hearing the phrase used by the boys of Hope come out of Calder's lips. That the phrase had survived both inside and outside of the shield was amazing. His amusement faded. It was odd that Calder had to go now.

And why would Calder lie about knowing Glenn?

19

ROSE

"Wake up." A distant voice called in Rose's mind.

She awoke to frigidly cold air and the feeling that her awareness extended past her physical body. There was a network beyond her that connected her to layers of undead. She could see out of thousands of eyes and feel the ground beneath thousands of feet. Worst of all, she could sense a small sliver of the person they had been. Panic filled her mind. Her heart struggled in her chest.

"Rose, your friends need you." The same voice that woke her said. "They're walking into a trap."

She strived to control her panic by taking a deep breath of the cold air and letting it out. That stilled the riot of feelings and thoughts in her head. She had to be strong for Daniel. She blocked out the other sensations and focused on her own body.

The extra awareness shrank until she lay on her side. The ground was cold beneath her cheek. The air was musty and still cold. She kept her eyes closed and focused on pushing against the stone floor. She swallowed and sat up slowly.

"What do I need to do?" Her voice sounded like a croak. She felt as if she were fighting her way out of cobwebs.

"You must control the undead to save your friends. It was just as you feared. Going near Hope put them in danger. The trap will be sprung before the night falls." The voice came from the far side of the room.

She jerked at the nearness of it. She hadn't sensed anyone in the room with her.

She opened her eyes and a man with a hawk nose and messy hair stood with his arms crossed. He looked familiar, but she couldn't place the memory. He didn't smell like anything. "Are you a ghost?"

He chuckled. "No, but I am not there with you. I am just a projection. I am with your friends. They need your help. Bring the undead down the tunnel."

Repugnance twisted her stomach. There was no way she was going to touch the threads that linked to all those undead. Some part of her knew it would be very dangerous and the experience could change her. She might never find her way back to herself. The voice could be lying and trying to trick her into this path.

"How do you know my friends?"

The not-ghost pursed his lips. "Max is there."

The image of Max sprang to mind. Confusion and unease twisted her gut. She remembered him. He was one of her best friends. He had the same nose and eyes as her dead husband.

The not-ghost sighed. "Joshua will be fighting for his life."

Rose's heart beat faster. Joshua was her best friend.

"And Serene..."

The pressure built in her chest. Serene had been the first one to know about being undead and had not only stood by her, but had helped her.

"And Master Phil will die."

Daniel.

She had to help no matter what it cost her. She'd never forgive herself if he—they died because she'd been too afraid of the consequences and risks.

"Follow my call once you're out of the tunnel," the projection said and then disappeared.

Rose put her feet on the ground. She had no idea how to control an undead army. The feeling when she had woken up had been overwhelming. Maybe if she reached out to just a few, she could figure out how to control them.

She took a breath and opened her mind to the undead near her. A dozen were pressed together, like sardines in a can, in a room down the hall, but each one couldn't see or sense the rest.

That was weird. What could prevent one undead from seeing another?

She first had to get the group out, and then would move them down the hall as the projection had said. If there was a trap, she needed to get to it first and disarm it. Barring that, she needed to rescue them. Worst case, she might have to fight using the undead.

She reached out to the place the voices came from. In each undead's core was a sliver of who they'd been in life. These slivers were tied into an energy she wanted nothing to do with and made her shiver. She very carefully touched the core of the one nearest to the door, avoiding the energy.

His name had been Fred. She could feel his body as he felt it. To him, his body was a suit that was too big, too heavy, and smothered him.

She had no idea what to do. How did she get Fred to do what she needed him to do? Fear of her friends dying soured her stomach. And there was something else that made her hesitate. It was the unfairness of it all.

Fred hadn't asked to be a zombie. Some force outside of him had forced a bit of his soul to stay behind. Just as she'd been forced into being an undead. She couldn't be that person. Not even to save her friends. She couldn't force, but perhaps she could ask.

"Fred? May I use your eyes and body to open the door?" she sent mentally to Fred.

She held her breath, waiting for his response. If he didn't give permission, she was done before she even started. Her friends would die if she couldn't bring them help, but the core of her knew it would be wrong to just use poor Fred. She'd reach out to the next zombie and the one after that until she found one who would work with her. If nothing else, she would bring herself and see if her training would allow her to find her opponent's weakest point and take advantage of it.

"Help me." Fred's voice was clear in her mind. In that instant, she knew what he wanted. He wanted to be free. It would make sense for all of the undead to be willing to help her if she helped them. She would have to release them from the energy that bound them to this place. She would have to release them.

"Agreed." She would do what she could to set them all free of the evil which kept them here.

A ripple went through the network at her agreement. Fred opened the door. Relief lightened her chest.

She touched the next zombie behind Fred. Her name had been Pauline. She set them both walking slowly down the hallway.

She connected four more, but then Fred got in trouble. The tunnel had turned and he kept going straight, banging into the wall again and again.

"Fred, stop!"

He did and stood there, waiting to be directed.

Pauline banged into Fred and the both landed in a pile on the floor. The next zombies fell over them as well.

Frustration and anger set fire to her chest and made her want to cry. How would this army help her if she had to tell each and every zombie to watch out for walls? Would the undead trip over bushes and fall down ravines too? She would spend all her time trying to move the zombies in trouble and not enough energy assessing the situation with her friends.

If she couldn't figure out how to get the zombies to be more self-directed, her friends would die. That's what the man she almost recognized had said.

The next zombie she mentally touched was different from Fred and Pauline and the others. The sliver of the person he had been was bigger and more defined. Luke's body felt like he was wearing a heavy coat.

"Luke, will you help me?"

"Yes. What do you need?" Luke asked back.

Rose gulped in surprise. Why had Luke's response been so much more coherent?

"I only died a few days ago," Luke responded. *"I still have the stuff they buried me with."* He took off the backpack he was wearing and showed her the contents. Thin rope and other metal objects filled his bag. The idea that Luke had his backpack was weird to Rose, but she had buried her husband with his favorite book.

Hope pulled hard at Rose's chest. If she could find enough zombies like Luke, she could use them to direct the older zombies. That would give her the extra time she needed to find out about the opponent. If she knew nothing about them, she couldn't use their strengths against them.

Rose also had no idea what lay ahead in the tunnel. Maybe Luke and his team could be her scouts.

"Can you help Fred and Pauline and the others to move as a unit

and avoid obstacles? The goal is to get out of the tunnel and get some intel on where we're going to come out."

"I can do that."

She could feel Luke's essence communicating with the others. Fred, Pauline, and the other four zombies tangled on the floor stood and followed Luke down the hall. They did it without the need for her to direct them.

Relieved, Rose sorted through the rest and found the ones who were more recently undead. She formed teams with the newest commanding the older ones, and then she put the freshest in charge of multiple teams. It was good Luke was on the scouting team, because he was the most recently dead and hopefully could recognize danger.

She gave the order for team after team to move forward. They went down the hallway faster. She told the commanders what she wanted. The zombies moved quicker and more easily. She just had to relay her desires down the ranks, and they did as she asked.

She sagged for a moment in relief. Once she got the zombies out of the tunnels she could locate her friends and protect them. She stood to follow.

"I have information," Luke said. She got an invite to look out of his eyes.

The tunnel came out by the river at the west side of town. Faintly on the other side of the channel, she could hear that man's voice. *"Hurry!"*

She knew the undead would cause panic if they were seen above ground. *"Is there any way across?"* she sent to Luke.

"No, there's just rushing water."

"Is there anything on the other side we can reach?" she asked him. The urgency of saving her friends was making her feel desperate. The undead could back up and try other tunnels and hope there was...what? A way across the water? She slumped.

The river would be there no matter where they might come out from the ravine. The running water cut New Nadezhda in half.

"Let me see it again?" Rose asked.

Luke let her view through his eyes again. The zombies stood by the water's edge. One of the zombies slipped and fell into the churning water. She lost touch with him as he rounded the next corner. The water was fast at this point. If they fell in, they would be sent out the other side of the town and who knows how far before they made it to the other side.

"How would you get across this if you were alive?" Rose asked.

"A bridge being out of the question?" Luke asked.

"Yes."

"If I were alive, I would use rope. See if I couldn't get across that way?" He sounded doubtful and unsure of his answer.

There was no way most of her zombies would be able to use a rope. Without her zombies able to cross the river soon, her friends would die.

20

ROSE

<u>Evening, Primum second, 300 years post-Merge</u>

Rose scanned the river again through Luke's eyes. All she saw was fast-moving water and rocks covered in slime. Slime that would be slippery for anyone and even worse for her zombies.

Despair crushed her chest like a weight.

She scanned again. What else could she do? There had to be a way to get her zombies across. The water was fast, but there were a few ripples that outlined things just under the surface. One odd ripple caught her eye. Instead of the turtle-back shape of the normal ripples, this one was narrower and taller. *"What's that?"*

Luke got closer, and she saw it was a plank. Excitement unfurled. *"Could it be a plank from a bridge?"*

"It could be. In fact, look at that structure there." He turned his head and pointed to a building she hadn't seen before. She had thought it was just random rocks and some sticks poking out,

but now she realized it was a bunch of boards heaped together. Her hope rose. If it was a bridge and enough of it was usable, she could get the zombies across.

"Want me to go check it out?" Luke asked.

"You can do that?" Rose asked, confused.

Luke took off his backpack, set it on the ground, and took out a thin rope and one of the metal objects he had shown her earlier. He flicked his wrist and the metal popped out and clicked. The item now looked like a set of metal claws.

"What is that?" Rose asked. She hadn't seen anything like it.

"A grappling hook. I can hook it onto the other side of the river and jump across." Luke sounded confident as he fed rope through a hole in the grappling hook and tied a knot. His hands fumbled a bit on the knot, but he seemed like he knew what he was doing.

"How do you know how to do that?"

He connected another rope to a tree and then tied that one on the grappling hook as well. *"I was a mountaineer before I died."*

Luke used to climb mountains? The hope surged hard within her chest. He might have the skills needed to get across the river. If they could get him across, the odds increased they could get the rest of the zombies across.

Luke swung the grappling hook high, seeming to be aiming for the remnants of the bridge. The hook connected with a metallic thunk. Was that a good thing? He pulled the rope and it held.

"What now?" Rose asked. Was he going to swing across like Tarzan?

"I swing."

She could feel his glee at the idea. *"You've done this before?"*

"What do you think I died of?" Luke grinned as he asked, and then he jumped.

Fear for him and what his not-death would mean to the mission flooded Rose. She disconnected and ran.

Her footsteps echoed wildly in the tunnel. She dodged past the slow-moving zombies still shambling forward. The narrow passage filled in with more and more zombies.

"I need to come through quickly." Rose sent to her commander zombies.

A narrow passage between the zombies opened, and she made it to the tunnel exit. Luke's team stood with their backs against the wall. The smell of fish and water hit her.

Where was Luke? She scanned the distant bank.

Across the way, he waved.

Relief made Rose laugh. She connected to Luke. *"You scared me."*

Luke chuckled. *"Let's hope it's a bridge."* He walked to the wall and tugged on the plank. It slipped out of his hands. He tugged again and pulled up the remains of a rope bridge. Ropes pulled away from the wall with a wet sucking sound but remained connected to the top where the grappling hook had connected.

Luke found the last plank and tied another rope to it. He dragged it across to the edge of the river.

"Think it will make it across?" Rose asked.

Luke shook his head and then pointed up behind her. Above her head were two dozen planks still dangling from where the bridge had connected to land.

Damn. Even if all of the boards had made it to the other side, there was no way the bridge would be long enough. She fought down her disappointment. There had to be something. *"Is there anything else over there that might be useful?"*

He picked his way across the rocks, falling occasionally. He went around the bend and out of her sight.

Rose checked her side of the river. She walked along the wall to look for anything that might help her get a zombie army across the river. Even another half of a bridge would be good.

Around the next bend, something white fluttered where it

was trapped in the rocks. She picked her way closer. The white was part of a rope net. It must not have been in the water long or it wouldn't be so white.

Rose slipped on a rock and slid into the cold water. The current pulled at her legs, but she was able to scramble back up. Getting over the rocks was definitely going to be a problem for the zombies.

Finding her balance, she untangled the net from around the rocks. The net was taller than she was. Many of the knots had come undone, so fish would slip right through. Zombies were bigger than most fish, so maybe she could use the net to haul them across the river. It wasn't like she had to worry about zombies drowning.

The only issue was that it would take a long time to haul a thousand zombies across the river. She was running out of time. Maybe there was another way to get the more coordinated ones across the river.

She picked up as much of the net as she could and walked back to the tunnel entrance.

Luke came back and lifted up more rope. *"I found a cave entrance this way."*

The plan snapped into place. First get the zombies over the river, and then into the cave, which hopefully led to where she needed to go to rescue her friends.

Maybe she could make a rope bridge for the more coordinated zombies. She envisioned a bridge strung close together along the bottom with two narrower strands about chest height.

"Can you tie the ropes on your side and throw the ends to me?" She sent Luke a mental picture of what she wanted to do.

He chuckled in her head and tied the ropes around some heavy debris. He went back to the rope attached to the grappling hook and untied the other line. He connected all three ropes to the line. *"Now you can pull them back."*

She went to the tree and pulled on the rope, bringing the tied ropes across the river with no issue. *"Thanks, Luke."*

She did her best to tie the ropes so she had a rope to walk across on the bottom and two to hang on to.

The team leads would cross first, and then she would haul their zombies across.

She took a breath and walked carefully across. The rushing water beneath her feet made her a little dizzy, so she focused on Luke standing on the far side. The rope swayed and her stomach twisted. If she was having this much trouble, how would the zombies feel? One thing at a time. She took a deep breath and thought about Daniel and her friends.

She stepped off the rope. The solid ground had never felt so good. *"Show me the cave."*

She followed Luke. There were dead fish and plants strewn between the rocks, which made it even harder to navigate than the other side. In one spot, a rock made a slippery ramp to the water. She had to hold on to the wall to keep from falling.

Around the corner was the cave. It was an actual tunnel leading away. Once she got the zombies across the river, the rocks would be too unsafe for most of her army.

She directed the team leads to cross the bridge. With each zombie who traversed, hope crowded her chest, but she still needed a way to get the main zombies across and up the bank on the other side.

It really was too bad the bridge hadn't been usable. That would have made things so much easier. The narrow planks reminded her of a fence... The idea exploded in her mind. She could use the bridge as a fence to catch the zombies and provide a handhold so they wouldn't end up in the river.

"Luke, I need help staking this. Then can you see about making the path to the cave easier to navigate?"

"I can do that."

She climbed up the wall to where the bridge still hung. She cut the ropes as close to the top as she could. The bridge clattered to the ground.

Luke took the end and had the rest of the zombies move the bridge to form a small alley between the rocky wall and the river.

She took a rock and banged on the top of one of the planks embedding it into the ground. They wouldn't be able to do that on all the planks, but hopefully they would be able to do it enough to stabilize the fence. She could have zombies hold the other end and brace too.

"Rose. The trap is almost sprung. We need you," that voice called in her head.

Fear and helplessness closed her throat and made it hard to breathe. There were still so many zombies standing on the other side. It was going to take hours to move them all. Daniel didn't have hours.

"If we tie them with a rope, we could get more across the bridge. The stronger ones could help the weaker ones across," Luke said.

But would it be fast enough to save her friends?

21

———

MAX

Max felt like they'd been walking for hours. The deeper he walked into the forest, the weirder he felt. The tingle of magic grew stronger with each passing moment. It had to be the shield.

The birds fell silent and so did the frogs and bugs. It was as if they were holding their collective breaths to see what happened.

"I have information for you. You must know what occurred." The soft voice was somewhere inside his head.

Max jumped and glanced around. Joshua was ahead. Serene and Master Phil must be farther ahead. The voice felt feminine, but no one near him was speaking. The voice was different from the zombies' voices. It was alive and desperate. Fear and curiosity tangled in his gut.

"Each book holds a promise of something new. A distillation of a story or of knowledge." He repeated what his teachers had said.

A feeling of profound sadness swamped him. *"My sister used to say that. Let me show you how it began,"* the voice whispered.

Sister? The tingle of magic that swirled around him seemed different. It was magic but not something he had felt before. *"How are you talking to me?"*

"It's my talent to be able to connect to others. Please, let me show you, and you will understand." The voice was coaxing, but he had the sense she would only use her magic to show him if he allowed her to.

"Why me?" He wondered why she didn't talk to Joshua or Serene. They would be much more able to help her.

"I can only reach someone near the shield, and we are distantly related."

Max hesitated to give her permission. He had no idea who she was or what her motivation for speaking to him was.

"What I want to show you may help save your friend."

If there was even a chance this information could help Rose, he would have to take the chance. *"Yes,"* he thought.

The world spun, and when he could see again, he was no longer Max. Feminine thoughts swirled around him. He wasn't sure how he knew, but the feeling was warmer and more fluid than what he normally felt. Her worry buffeted him. He wasn't her. The experience was more like watching a movie through her eyes and experiencing her thoughts and feelings in the moment.

She walked up a road carrying a bag. He knew there were spell supplies in that bag. Just like he knew her name was Ember.

He turned her name over in his mind. One of the sisters who had founded Hope had been named Ember. It had been hundreds of years since the town had been founded; she would be long gone from this world.

Ember turned back to look at the town. Hope lay below in a

slight valley. It looked different than it had when he'd last looked back. There were buildings missing and the road was paved with a black substance.

Farmland in a lush green extended toward the town. The sun was setting. He felt a strange foreboding overtake her, sending chills up her spine. This would be the last time she saw Hope. The spell they were doing to protect the town would be her last.

Ember shivered. It wasn't like her to have premonitions. That was more Calder's area. She was a psychic able to speak telepathically.

Worry pulled Max back from the vision. Calder had been one of the brothers who had founded the town. Hope looked so different through her eyes, perhaps it was a memory from long ago. None of this could be relevant to today.

"What's going on?" Max asked in his head.

"Hush, you'll see," Ember scolded.

The scene changed and two men with hawk noses and messy hair stood by the road waiting for her. She had the equipment they needed to cast the spell, and time was running out.

Calder ran his hand through his hair and huffed impatiently. When he turned toward Ember, Max flinched. His eyes were identical to the Calder he knew. It had to be the same man.

The other man grinned at Ember, which sent a surge of love through her.

"Glenn," Ember sent to him.

Max could feel the current of love that flowed between Ember and Glenn. They must be soul-bonded.

"Calder and Yaneli were as well," Ember's voice whispered.

There couldn't be many Yanelis, so Ember must be talking about the Mistress Yaneli who had sent both Max and Rose on the quest to take down the shield. He had no idea how she could be in this vision.

"How long do we have?" Yaneli sounded exasperated.

"My sister would much rather be in her study instead of out in the 'wild.'" Ember's voice told him.

This Yaneli was younger and innocent looking, while the Mistress Yaneli he knew was scarred across the face, and her one good eye looked as if she had suffered some kind of trauma. There was no mistaking, though, that they were the same woman.

"Wait," Max said. *"Are you saying the Mistress of Hope, the undead expert from the council, you, and the man who has been poisoning Rose were the ones who put up the shield?"* Stunned disbelief had him pulling away. It didn't seem possible the founders of Hope could still be alive.

"Please wait. You need to understand," Ember's voice insisted.

What could any of this have to do with Rose? Ember must want something. But what?

The emotions had felt so real, and the view of Hope had been different than what he would've conjured if it had been his own imagination. There was so much he didn't know, and maybe Ember really did have clues as to what happened to Rose.

"You will understand soon," Ember said.

He immersed himself in the vision and felt time passing in fast forward. The stars twinkled in the night sky above. Ember inscribed a spell circle in the ground, dividing it into four equal parts. In each of the parts, she drew the symbol for earth, air, fire, or water.

When Ember completed her task, she stood and stretched. *"Are you almost ready?"* she sent telepathically to Glenn.

"Yes, my love. Just one more thing to get," Glenn replied.

Yaneli stood on the far side of the circle and stared back toward the town. She pulled at her lip and seemed paler than

Ember had ever seen her. Worry for her sister and the feeling that something was wrong grew.

"Did you have a message for me to pass to Yaneli? She's getting nervous," Ember sent.

"Isn't she always?" Glenn sent a blast of his love, warming her. *"It will be okay. You know I will protect you with my last breath."*

Ember hugged Glenn, feeling his essence surrounding her. They would face whatever was to come together.

Her sister being nervous and ambitious was not anything new. It was consistent with the air element she corresponded to, just as Ember's temper, and Glenn's stability drew from their guiding element.

The ceremony started, but Max was drawn away from the details. *"It would not be good for you to know how we did this,"* Ember said to Max.

Max knew most magical spells involved precise movements, chanted words, and ingredients. A spell like putting up a shield that had lasted hundreds of years had probably taken hours. He'd rather watch paint dry.

The scene established itself with the mages each in their own part of the spell circle. Their hands were linked and their heads bowed. The last notes of the spell fell away.

Ember could feel the bubble surrounding them. It was strong and true. They'd done it. They'd saved Hope from destruction. Elation and relief filled her. She could feel Glenn's excitement.

"We did it," she sent to him.

A snap and crackle and the feeling that something was very wrong made her bones twinge. The feeling came from the shield.

Calder's head snapped up. "The shield is breaking. We have to reinforce it."

"What can we do?" Glenn asked.

"If we go outside, we can stabilize the magic." Calder stood and moved as if he were pushing through water. "Yaneli, come with me."

Ember felt a stab of panic. "Calder, you need a different element to stabilize your water or you'll overwhelm the shield."

"She's right. Glenn is earth, he should help you," Yaneli said.

Glenn stood and the two brothers walked out of the spell circle and to the edge of the shield.

"Be careful," Ember sent.

Glenn caught her gaze, nodded, and sent a rush of love.

"We need to reinforce the inside." Yaneli stood and put her foot in the section of the spell circle her husband had been in. Ember stood and put her foot in the earth section.

"We got the shield up just in time. I can feel the world ripping apart." Glenn's mental voice shook. His fear and awe were evident in his tone. She wondered what it looked and felt like for him to be that affected.

Ember added her strength to repair the inner cracks.

"I wish you could see the colors and the magic. It's like a giant is shredding the world," Glenn's voice continued. *"We have a few cracks left to fill. The outside spell is at the shift point. It must have been too much for the shield."*

Ember patched the crack. There were two more on the inside. Anything between the two surfaces would heal once they got the inner and outer walls done.

"The buildings and trees are floating. Gravity has no meaning here." Glenn sent an image of orange lines crisscrossing the sky. A medieval castle popped into existence.

Fear for him made her ask, *"How are you surviving?"*

"We created another smaller shield on the outside." Glenn reassured her. *"It looks like whoever did this spell merged other dimensions together. The magic in the air is heavier than even in our sacred place on our sacred day."*

Shock coursed through Ember. The four of them had been the most potent concentration of power on record. If this event was more powerful, then they needed to get the shield fixed so Hope would survive.

The crack she patched ripped open. *"It keeps breaking."* She looked up at Yaneli who looked just as worried as she felt. "The cracks I fix keep reopening."

"Mine too," Yaneli said softly.

"Calder thinks it's one big crack, and we have to each perform the repair at the same time," Glenn said.

"The guys think we need to fix the crack at the same time. You ready? On the count of three." Ember glanced over at Yaneli. A flash of jealousy crossed her sister's face. She'd always resented Ember's ability to talk telepathically to Glenn.

Yaneli nodded.

"We are ready," Ember said to Glenn. *"On the count of three."*

"One," Ember said. *"One."*

She focused on the crack and readied her energy.

"Two," Ember said. *"Two."* She could feel Yaneli's focus as well.

"Ready," Glenn sent.

"Three," Ember said. *"Three."*

Ember patched the last crack and could feel the added energy of them all patching at the same time. The shield solidified under her mental hand. The moment of elation was swamped by pain. Her body felt as if she were being torn in two. She hunched over, trying to locate the attack. It was the soul-bond, torn. Glenn was no longer a part of her.

Pain, shock, and confusion stormed Ember's body.

"He's gone." Her sister fell to her knees, and a sob wrenched out of her throat.

Ember fought her way free of the feelings. She hadn't felt Glenn die, she had felt the bond break. Maybe he was just on the other side of the shield. She grabbed on to the idea. The thought of him being alive sparked and pushed down the rest of her feelings and the vast emptiness the broken soul-bond left. "They're still there. They're just on the other side of the shield."

Yaneli nodded, and tears streaked across her face. "Can you feel them?"

Ember reached out with her senses and realized she couldn't go past the shield. Her husband could be on the other side. She took a step closer to the shield. Something about the way it felt to her mental probing seemed off. "The shield feels strange. There's a reflective feel to it."

Her sister looked away, but not before the expression on her face gave away she knew the shield was different.

"What did you do to the shield? There is magic there that shouldn't be there." A rush of urgency hit Ember. She had to understand what had happened in order to get to her husband.

"We just added some extra protection." Yaneli didn't look at Ember when she said it. This was a sure sign she was lying.

Ember read the magic. "The shield gives you control over the people and something else." Shock and worry churned her stomach. If she couldn't get through, the soul-bond would be gone for good. Glenn and she would be separated, even in the next life.

"It will concentrate the magic talent. Make more people be born with the gift."

Ember read the magic and saw what her sister said was true, but it also would give them control. "It would give you power."

"And help humanity. Magical people were not meant to be outcasts." Yaneli finally sounded like her scornful self.

"But it backfired. It won't allow anyone with magic to cross. Were you going to take down the shield or were you going to leave it up so you could control the people of Hope?"

Her sister didn't respond, but her face said it all. Controlling the people in Hope had been the plan. Calder and Yaneli had probably been waiting for a way to make this happen. The people would be grateful to them and would give them whatever they wanted.

There was one more part of the spell she didn't understand. All of them were bound to the shield. "And you would live forever." The last Ember said in a strangled whisper.

Calder and Yaneli had miscalculated. The men were outside the shield with no way to get back inside. Her soul-bond was broken because of her sister, and if she read the spell right, they were all connected to the shield and would live forever. Forever without Glenn.

"It's not right." Ember could feel her temper flare. She struggled to control it. Losing her focus wouldn't help Glenn.

"We needn't talk about that now. What we need to do is see if we can get the men across." Yaneli's voice broke.

The ache in Ember's soul throbbed at the thought of her husband. Her sister was right. She stood up, dusted herself off, and helped Yaneli stand.

They walked closer to the barrier, Ember refrained from touching it and tried to feel her way between the layers of the shield. "I'm not seeing any way through. What do you think of..."

A push on her back sent Ember face first into the shield. Ember's magic flared reflectively at the attack, and Yaneli screamed.

Ember couldn't think about Yaneli's pain; she could feel the magic ripping her essence apart. Fear and desperation had her reaching out with her powers. Instead of trying to force her way through the barrier, she merged herself with the protective layer. It was just another psychic connection.

Her body fell away and her spirit entered the shield.

Ember looked back through the shield and saw her sister on her hands and knees. Her face and one shoulder were charred and blistered. "You won't interfere with the plan, sister." The last part was spat out.

Ember made her way through the magic to the other side. Now that she was in spirit form, she was able to navigate to the outer edge that touched the world outside.

"Glenn?" She called out tentatively, stretching out beyond the barrier. She couldn't reach very far.

"My love?" His voice sounded heavy with grief. She mentally reached for him as she had so many times, and she could feel the soul-bond reestablish. Relief almost broke her concentration.

"What happened? Are you safe?" he asked. *"I felt the bond break."*

"The shield. Calder and Yaneli added something to it. It broke our bond."

"How did you get past it?"

"I-I'm in the shield now." Ember sent him a vision of what had happened with Yaneli and what she'd discovered about the magic.

"You will die without the shield," Glenn sent. His feeling of betrayal and loss and the underlying fear of never seeing Ember again made her shiver. *"I will hide the shield to protect you."*

Now Max returned to himself. Having experienced the story himself, he believed her. He had felt the push and the feeling of betrayal. That was why no one on the outside had ever found the barrier. It had been hidden all these years by Glenn, who was kept alive by his connection to the magic.

"Why are you telling me this?" Max asked.

"You need to take down the shield." Under her words was a strange feeling of resignation he didn't understand.

"You'll die."

She laughed with no humor. *"No human was meant to live this long. And the loss of a soul-bond is horrible enough to experience once."*

Remembering when she told him that distance from the shield was part of why she had picked him, Max realized the soul-bond must re-break every time Ember went to the other end of the shield to spy on her sister or see if Glenn left the shield's area. *"What about Glenn?"*

"The man I love wouldn't have poisoned anyone. Losing the bond so many times has changed him. Twisted him." Ember's tone was full of conviction. *"I have to hope that in our next reincarnation, we will be together."*

Her presence left him as he stepped into a small clearing. Now that she was gone, the hairs on his arms rose. The shield was nearby. His whole body knew it.

Joshua, Serene, and Master Phil, in their human forms, stood on a stump that rose out of the middle of the clearing. The tree must have been ancient and massive.

Max stepped onto the stump. The top was flat and was wider than a small house. Powerful magic had been used in this place over the years. The feel of it sent a chill down his spine. The information Ember had given him didn't sit well and didn't help him find Rose.

If what Ember had said was correct, then Calder did know Glenn. They were brothers. Why would Calder come with them to find Glenn, and how did Rose fit in?

"There's something odd in the woods." Serene stepped closer to Max and lowered her voice. "I've never gone this direction before."

"Me neither." Joshua took out his bow and with the way he moved, Max realized this man was a deadly hunter. "What do you sense?"

"Ancient magic here..." She gestured ahead. "And strange magic that way."

"It's the shield." Max was sure of that.

"That makes sense. There's something else out there," Serene said.

Joshua nodded, and then he, too, seemed to concentrate. "There are many watching us in the woods. The animals are too interested," he said in a distant voice. "Whatever it is I sense is hanging back."

Max tried to use his senses to figure out what was going on. He could smell the animals of the forest. There was also the human they'd been tracking nearby.

He glanced up at Serene who nodded subtly. She knew that Glenn was near.

Max stepped closer and lowered his voice. "I don't smell Rose at all."

"We couldn't smell her when she fled earlier. I'm not giving up hope." Serene squeezed his shoulder. "We'll find her."

"Where's Calder?" Joshua asked.

"He went to water a tree." Max shook his head.

Joshua frowned and shot a puzzled look at Serene. Her shrug confused Max until he realized that Calder knowing the phrase was additional proof he was from Hope. It meant what Ember had said was true. He needed to let Joshua, Serene, and Master Phil know what he'd found out.

"I had something—"

"Who trespasses in my wood?" A deep masculine voice boomed from the tree line.

22

MAX

Max jerked. His heart thumped. He scanned the area, but didn't see anyone. Out of the corner of his eye he saw Joshua and Serene crouch.

The feeling of the woods darkened as if a storm were brewing. Assuming the deep voice belonged to Glenn, how could he get the man to show himself? Surely seeing him would tell Max if he had Rose. He felt like he was still missing so many pieces of the puzzle.

Maybe the direct approach was better. Glenn didn't know that they knew he had tried to poison Rose. "We are friends of Rose," Max said loudly.

"Indeed," the booming voice said. "Why are you here?"

What could Max say to that? He didn't want to admit to knowing Glenn had been poisoning Rose. He wasn't sure mentioning the vision from Ember would help either. Maybe he could admit Rose was missing. Max had no idea why Glenn was poisoning Rose or who had taken her. Unless both events had to do with her being able to hear the undead.

But even that didn't make a whole lot of sense. He could hear the undead, so why hadn't they taken him? Someone had, and that was why he was missing memories. The flash of graves came back to him. He shook off the feeling.

Why would Glenn care about the ability to hear undead? If Ember was right, all Glenn cared about was keeping his wife safe in the shield.

"Rose is gone." Max held back the rest of the details he might give to see what the man had to say.

"I'm sorry to hear about her death." The voice still boomed but sounded sad. Had he just admitted to poisoning her? Maybe the sadness was manufactured.

"She's not dead. She was taken," Max said.

"T-taken?" Ahead, the leaves rustled and the branches parted. A tall man with a hawk nose, a slightly older, more unkempt version of Glenn from the vision, stepped out. His eyes were different from the vision. The edge of madness glinted in them. "What happened?"

"We think you have her." Max watched Glenn closely. If Max was lucky, he'd be able to tell if that were true.

Glenn's eyes widened. Then slowly he shook his head, with his brow furrowed as if he were deep in thought. "I couldn't take her."

Couldn't was an odd phrase. "Why not?"

"It would have put everything at risk." Glenn focused his gaze on each of them in turn. Max got his attention last. "You're from Hope. You crossed the shield five years ago."

Max started. How could the man know that? Dread pooled in his stomach, but he had to ask. "What happened?"

Glenn shrugged. "You were out of my range before I could reach you." He gazed at Max with what almost looked like sympathy. "You know what it is like to lose the woman you love."

Max reeled back. He felt a crack inside of his memory, and an image of Rose walking away from him filled his mind. He hadn't wanted to go back into his house because he'd known what he would find. Eleanor dying. He struggled against the grief the thought and partial memory gave him. He pushed it into a mental box and sat on it. If he didn't, then Rose and his friends would die.

Glenn gave him a small smile. "And why have you come to see me?"

Max didn't care about this man's crimes. He knew Rose was in danger, and somehow this man was involved. Maybe if he could find out what Glenn knew, he'd get another clue about where Rose was.

"You gave her potions," Max said. Because he had been watching, Max caught the subtle flinch. Did that mean he regretted poisoning Rose, or he regretted he was caught?

"The potions were to keep away the voices." He pulled on his beard and frowned.

Max glanced at Joshua, whose attention was focused on Glenn. Serene and Daniel must have slipped away. How could he keep Glenn talking?

"She ran from me as if the very gates of hell were opened and the whole host of demons were on her tail," Max said.

Glenn's expression morphed to one of dismay and fear. "Then we are all in grave danger." Glenn turned to Joshua. "I know you. You do good work for the HPA. You've upheld justice and kept the peace. All of that is in danger now."

"What do you mean?" Max asked. "What does any of this have to do with Rose?"

"There is another who would use her powers to form an undead army. We must keep her away from him." Every word vibrated with Glenn's sincerity.

Calder had said Glenn wanted the army. "We were told you were raising an undead army," Max said.

"No." The man looked despondent. He tugged on his beard. "I only poisoned her because it was the only way to make sure she didn't fall into his hands."

Could the "he" he spoke of be Calder?

"She was stronger than you thought," Max said. How long had Glenn been poisoning Rose?

"Indeed."

"Tell us about this other man. He might have her. We need to find him and rescue Rose," Max said.

At that moment, Calder stepped out from the brush. "Hello, brother." His voice sneered.

The word 'brother' smacked Max in the face. Calder saying that made everything Max had seen in the vision feel more real. Calder stepped from the path between the trees and held up his hands.

Max gasped and staggered back. Calder was in the stance Max had seen the mages in Hope assume when they were about to duel. Fear tightened his stomach. He had to get Joshua away. Now. Dueling mages were wild and unpredictable. Depending on what their talents were, they could fight with anything. He'd seen a duel between lightning and fire once. All the houses nearby had been destroyed. The trees thrashed in the wind that kicked up.

"Take cover!" Max shouted and dove off the stump. The tingle of magic pulsed up his body, and the smell of burnt wood hit him hard.

Black smoke smoldered from a depression where he'd been standing.

"You led him here. Secrecy was the best protection." Glenn made another gesture and a bolt of lightning hit Calder in the chest, leaving behind a cloud of smoke.

"Now that I know where the barrier is, I can finally take it down." The smoke cleared, revealing Calder unharmed.

Max backed away. Maybe while the men were distracted, he could look for Rose.

"No, you can't." Glenn visibly swallowed and then lifted his chin. "Ember is in there."

Max made it to the brush line.

Calder laughed in a way that sent shivers down Max's spine.

"Do you think I believe your lies?" Calder asked. "Your wife is dead."

Joshua came out of the shadows next to Max. His bow was out, but he hadn't taken a shot. Suddenly, Serene stood next to him and watched the fight.

There was something odd in the way the mages held themselves. Like they were trying to parse through and locate the truth. Max wasn't sure who to help either. Neither man seemed good. And there was little he could do in a wizard duel.

"Ember's alive," Glenn snarled. "And I'll not let you kill her."

"I'm sorry that it has come to this, brother, but we must free the people of Hope," Calder said. He raised his hands and began to chant.

"I expected you would find me sometime. Rise, my children." Glenn made a gesture with both hands, like he was waving people to come closer. The tingle of magic went through Max.

A stag came out to the left of Calder and knocked him off his feet.

"Glenn has control of the animals." Max stumbled back. A wave of small birds fluttered and darted near his head. The bite of their tiny beaks startled him. He waved his arms to ward off the attack. He stepped back and tripped over a hole. It hadn't been there a moment before. A tiny mole poked its head up and then scurried back underground.

The gut-wrenching roar of an enraged bear sounded. They were in trouble.

23

ROSE

<u>Evening, Primum second, 300 years post-Merge</u>

The forest felt strange to Rose. It wasn't the silent trees that stood like guardians along the path that freaked her out. There was a tension she didn't understand. A tug in her chest compelled her toward Hope. The sensation was as powerful as the fear used to be. And it was only getting stronger.

Worry pooled in her gut. She was going to rescue her friends from a trap, but the closer she got to the source of the pull, the more she questioned the wisdom of her actions. How did the not-ghost who looked so familiar know about the trap?

She realized that even if she'd wanted to, she might not be able to resist the urgency of force compelling her forward. The pull became more frantic and pushed the zombie army faster than she'd thought possible.

Everything in her knew time was running out. If she didn't get there soon, everyone she loved would die.

The zombies spread out, all heading toward the source of the compulsion. Because it had taken her so long to get them all across, Luke's group was the first to reach the goal.

"Rose, you have to see this," Luke sent.

She stopped her run to look through Luke's eyes.

Daniel, Max, Serene, Joshua, and a man she didn't recognize were fighting off an animal army. Fear set her heart racing. Was she too late?

Luke turned his head so she could see the squirrels leaping from the trees and scratching Joshua. The birds swarmed, pecking and flapping in Max's face. A stag rushed Serene and Daniel, who switched to furred form and scattered. On the ground, another person writhed beneath a bear that stood on its hind legs as it attacked the man she didn't know.

"Protect me," the voice screamed in her head. It came from the man on the ground.

"Calder's the one who woke us up," Luke sent with a hint of anger.

Rose's stomach dropped. Was the undead expert the council had sent to the cemetery behind the rise in undead?

Daniel yelped as another stag caught him with his rack.

There were so many animals. The zombies would be ineffective against them. The animals were too fast, and there were too many of them. A direct assault wouldn't help her friends. There had to be someone controlling the animals?

She sent out the word to surround the area and look for another person.

"Here," Fred called.

Rose switched her perspective and looked out of Fred's eyes.

Fred was at the edge of a clearing. The glistening shield was just beyond. A bubble of surprise and unease stung her chest.

A man sat outside the shield, swaying back and forth and muttering to himself. He held what looked like a charm in his hand. She couldn't see his face because his hair fell forward and covered it, but something about him seemed familiar. Could he be the source of the attack?

She switched back to Luke's view and saw that Joshua and Serene were standing back-to-back and fighting. They had numerous cuts and Serene looked worried. Joshua didn't, but Rose knew him well enough to know he rarely looked worried.

Daniel limped forward in wolf form and snapped at the birds attacking Max.

Through Luke's ears she heard a slight sound and through his eyes looked up to see a large mountain lion ready to pounce on Daniel and Max.

She had no way of helping them. Even Luke would be too slow.

If she was right and the muttering man was controlling the animals, then if she could break his concentration, that could break the spell.

If he knew she was attacking, he would pull his animal forces back and focus on that attack and stop them. Which would be good for Max and Daniel, but not good for her. She could send a zombie, but she wasn't sure any zombie could hold the man. Maybe if she could send in most of her zombies to help her friends, and Fred and Luke to attack the man? Then, if she ran in and grabbed him, she could break his concentration. From the wizards from Hope, she knew holding him might not be enough.

It was worth the risk.

She sent Fred in to grab the man and sprinted to where Fred was.

Fred had fallen on the man. He cursed and rolled over, pushing Fred away.

Rose knocked the charm out of the man's hand and grabbed his arms.

"Noooooo," he shrieked. He bucked away, almost breaking her grip. She hadn't expected him to do that, but her training took over and she turned him, using his own arms to wrap around his torso.

He threw his head back and screamed, twisting his body and just missing slamming his head into her face. She held on, barely able to keep him controlled.

"Luke, be my eyes."

She looked out Luke's eyes and saw the animals retreating. The birds were the first to flutter away. Then the smaller animals. The mountain lion yawned and stalked deeper into the woods.

Finally, the bear snorted and went back on all fours. Rose stopped the zombies from attacking the retreating animals.

The man in her arms arched and screamed like a wounded animal. Rose let him go before he could hurt himself or her. He landed in a heap on the ground. He looked up at her, and brushed the hair from his face.

"Glenn?" She stared at him in shock. "W-what?"

Calder stormed forward and snatched the necklace from Glenn's neck. There was a burst of light and the necklace transformed into a stone necklace.

"I finally have what I need to take down the shield." Calder held the necklace up like a trophy.

"No! You will kill her," Glenn cried out.

"Hold him," Calder commanded.

Rose grabbed Glenn and held him. Something about the desperation in Glenn's voice made her question her actions. "Who do you think we'll kill?" Rose asked. Glenn had always been so kind to her. He had given her potions for the voices. Confusion made her head hurt.

"My wife, Ember," he pleaded. He looked desperate. His hair and eyes were wild and spit ran from his mouth. He looked nothing like the cool, calm, collected man she had met to obtain potions to diminish the voices for all of those years.

"She's dead already. She died three hundred years ago," Calder sneered. "And now I will finally be able to reconnect with my wife."

24

MAX

Evening, Primum second, 300 years post-Merge

Max slumped near the shield. The zombies had defeated the wild creatures. Rose still stood apart and still held on to Glenn. He should be excited or at the very least relieved, but Rose had a strange, vacant look on her face. She hadn't reacted to her friends being there and had jumped to Calder's command. He must be imagining it.

"Help me," Master Phil asked as he struggled to get a bandage on his arm.

Max went to help him. As soon as he stepped near, Master Phil said, "There's still something wrong." Master Phil's voice was soft and urgent. His gaze darted to Rose.

"We still don't know who was controlling her." Max pitched his voice low. He thought of what Valeria had said about two different people or factions with opposite goals. "My money is on the brothers."

Master Phil gave him a puzzled look, so Max quickly filled him in on Ember's vision.

"So Glenn and Calder are brothers." Master Phil nodded and seemed deep in thought. "If we are going to conspire, you should know my real name. Call me Daniel."

A warm feeling spread in Max's chest at Daniel's acceptance. "I have a bad feeling about this. The undead army came in handy with the animals, but..." Max wasn't sure how to finish that sentence. Everything felt wrong. They'd found Rose, but nothing had changed.

"There is a bigger game afoot." Daniel glanced again at Rose. His eyes were worried.

It hadn't changed because Rose was still being controlled. Max lowered his voice even more. "What happened to Wren and Valeria?"

Daniel looked away from Rose. "They couldn't get the spell circle to be truly portable. I've been going back to them and bringing them closer. They'll need some time for set-up."

"And we still have to get Rose to the spell circle," Max said.

Max guessed that once the spell circle was set, it couldn't be moved. Rose didn't seem to be in any hurry to move. Calder had been lying this whole time. Glenn hadn't been any better, since he tried to poison Rose. Perhaps Calder had threatened Glenn with an undead army. He thought back to the vision Ember had given him. Yaneli had pushed her own sister through the shield. She had been soul-bonded to Calder. Maybe they were both bad people. Something about that felt right. At least it supported Max's feeling that Rose was still in trouble.

The only way things went back to right was if they could get the control element off Rose. "You need to tell Valeria and Wren to start preparations."

Daniel glanced at Rose again and nodded. "I'll slip away now." Daniel stepped back toward the trees.

Max walked to Joshua and Serene to draw attention away from Daniel. They were both watching Calder mutter as he kept glancing at the shield.

"What is he doing?" Max gestured toward Calder.

"Waiting for something." Joshua and Serene were much more subtle, but they also cast occasional glances in Rose's direction.

Max quietly told them what Ember had shown him and about Daniel getting Valeria and Wren ready.

"Losing a bond. How horrible." Serene shuddered.

Joshua put his arm around her. "I bet it was."

Max realized that they weren't just talking about the couples' broken soul-bonds, but something Serene had gone through.

"Do we help Calder?" Serene asked.

If the shield was the reason for the sickness in Hope, then it had to come down. "I think the shield needs to come down." He didn't say he wasn't sure what would happen once the shield went down.

Something moved on the other side of the shield. It was Mistress Yaneli. She walked like a predator and stared hungrily at Calder.

As if he could feel her regard, Calder rose and turned toward her. He took a step forward. His arms raised as if to embrace her, then he stopped. "Can you hear me, my love?"

Mistress Yaneli shook her head. Her lips moved, but no sound penetrated the shield.

Calder lifted his hand and showed her the necklace he'd taken from Glenn. Mistress Yaneli smiled, looking relieved. She raised her hand to show him her own necklace. Max stepped closer and saw it was a fire symbol.

"We can take down the shield." Calder laughed.

"What can we do to help?" Max asked.

Calder jerked as if he had forgotten Max was there. His wild expression was replaced with the bland one he'd been using all trip. "Make sure no one touches me."

Max stepped back and stood next to Rose. As he got closer, he saw how haunted her eyes were. Her expression reinforced the feeling that Rose was in trouble.

Calder cleared his throat and started to sing. He raised the necklace in his right hand. Mistress Yaneli raised the necklace in her right hand as well and her lips moved as if she sang. Their movements mirrored each other.

The shield shimmered.

Glenn flinched in Rose's grasp. "Ember?" he whispered.

"*Thank you,*" Ember's voice whispered to Max.

The shield popped, sending a wave of power through Max. The force tingled along his skin. The next shockwave knocked him to his knees.

A desperate scream caught Max's attention. Rose had a man he recognized as an older Glenn in one of her fancy holds. Glenn twisted just as the next shockwave hit. Rose fell just as Max had, and Glenn twisted free, his arm dangling useless and injured.

"You killed her!" Glenn charged at Calder. Murderous intent shone in his glare.

Calder stepped away and kicked Glenn as he went by. "Oh brother, we meant to kill you both years ago." Calder put the glowing necklace over Mistress Yaneli's head.

Mistress Yaneli laughed, sounding like a witch from the old movies they'd watched. Her scars twisted with each breath. Her face transformed until she looked like evil incarnate. How had Max ever believed she had cared about him or Hope?

Glenn growled and pulled out a knife. His eyes glittered in desperate rage. "Because of your greed I lost her."

"Come, brother. Make me pay for my sins," Calder sneered.

Glenn roared and charged. Calder stepped out of the way,

grabbed the knife, and plunged it into Glenn's chest.

Calder tossed Glenn away as if he were rubbish and turned to embrace Mistress Yaneli.

Sympathy for the man Ember had shown Max made him kneel by the dying man. "Ember is waiting for you."

Glenn opened his eyes, which were now clear. "Tell Rose I'm sorry." He struggled to breathe for a moment longer.

Rose stood beside him, and tears ran down her face.

"What's wrong?" Max asked, and a feeling of dread crept up his back.

"I'm not sure we did the right thing." Rose said it quietly, but it was as if she had shouted.

Calder and Mistress Yaneli turned toward her. The dread in Max's back deepened its hold. He had the urge to put himself between Rose and the couple, but the realization that he was overmatched by these very powerful mages stopped him.

"You're right." Calder smiled at Rose. "Rose, Rose. You must accept your fate." Calder shook his head in mocking sadness.

Rose shook her head to deny his words. She covered her ears and her expression twisted as if she was in pain. He'd seen that look on her face when she'd screamed, "Noooo!" in Daniel's house.

"You know how to make it stop," Calder purred. "Just give in."

Max cast a look toward Joshua and Serene in the hopes they had some idea how to save Rose. Joshua must have communicated something to Serene with his eyes, because she backed into the shadows and was gone.

"No." Rose groaned. Max looked back at Rose's agonized face.

"I made you, and you will obey me," Mistress Yaneli said.

Rose froze, and her eyes rolled back until only the whites showed. Fear for Rose clogged his throat.

Rose slowly stood. Her eyes looked as vacant as they had when she had run away from Daniel's house. She was lost.

25

ROSE

<u>Evening, Primum second, 300 years post-Merge</u>

Rose retreated into herself. Panic spread through her. What was happening to her? How could she fight something she didn't understand? The answer had to be in Hope.

She sought back in her memory for her last memory there.

Rose was at the top of the stairs in the mansion looking across the fancy parlor at a woman reclining on a settee. She was a delicate, fine-boned beauty in a green velvet gown. The table next to her held enough food to feed a family.

A strange resentment filled Rose's belly. This was not what she had expected of the town protector. Had everything she'd been told been a lie?

Mistress Yaneli took the white, lace-trimmed handkerchief away from her cheek. Scars marred one side of her face and one eye was entirely white. She'd been seriously burned in the past.

"Rose, how nice of you to join me." The woman looked her up and down. "I need you to go on a mission for me."

The feeling of wrongness prevailed on Rose. "Ma'am, my kids are alone now. I need to get back to tend them."

"I see." The woman tapped her red lips with the tip of her finger. And then she smiled. The smile didn't look kind or friendly, but instead reminded Rose of the pictures of wolves with their teeth bared. "Let me put this in terms you will understand. If you don't help me, your children will suffer."

Mistress Yaneli would kill her children. She backed up a step at the hostility in Mistress Yaneli's voice.

"If you do help me, I will see that your children are well taken care of."

Rose gulped and considered her options. She could get her kids and hide.

"If you're plotting to run away, know that Ferrik is already bringing your children here."

Rose's heart dropped. That's why he'd said he was sorry. That's why he'd said he'd do what he could. If Mistress Yaneli had Rose's children, she would be forced to help.

Mistress Yaneli's look of triumph made Rose feel cornered. She had no choice. This town was run by this woman. There was nowhere Rose could hide. She was literally trapped within a bubble. Feeling overwhelmed, she took the only option she could. "What do you need me to do?"

"Drink this and cross the shield."

Mistress Yaneli snapped her fingers in front of Rose's face, pulling her from the memory. "I need you to prove your loyalty."

Rose's stomach felt heavy. Here she was again, trapped with no options. But this time she knew Mistress Yaneli would hurt those Rose loved.

Mistress Yaneli grinned at Rose. "Kill..." She pointed at Max.

"Him. That will prove to me your children were worth keeping this whole time."

Rose's throat closed. Were her children really alive? She'd thought they were dead, but she had no memory of them dying. But to kill Max...

Mistress Yaneli handed Rose a stake. "Now."

Rose's gaze moved to Max. He was family and one of the best friends she had ever had. She couldn't kill him. But if her children were alive and Rose didn't do as Mistress Yaneli bade, Rose had no doubt her children would die slow, painful deaths.

Rose could hear the voices of the nearby dead. She'd caught the look that had passed between Joshua and Serene and knew Serene had gone for help.

The HPA had protocols for out-of-control wizards. The key was not getting killed in the first encounter, and living long enough to summon the other wizards who could handle the rogue. Joshua was hidden in the brush nearby, hopefully waiting for a chance to rescue her. She needed to delay as long as she could and do as little damage as possible.

Mistress Yaneli twisted something inside Rose that made her body shudder with pain and stars explode before her eyes. She wished she could warn Joshua away. There would be no saving her.

She had to obey, but she needed to do something to give Max a chance. If he could get away, then maybe he could save her children or help the city she had grown to love defend itself. He could be a valuable ally because he knew her. He knew how she thought and maybe that would help him defend against the attack Mistress Yaneli had ordered.

Rose had the zombie nearest Max grab him. He didn't struggle. His chin was up, and he stared her down. His eyes said he loved her like a sister and was willing to give up his life for her.

"Do it!" Mistress Yaneli screamed and tightened the reins of control on Rose.

Rose closed her eyes and took a shaky breath. She knew her children were either dead or in grave danger. Killing Max wouldn't change that. He was undead, just as she was. She recognized that fact now. And if she stabbed him soon, she would have control over where she stabbed him. If she did it right, he'd have a chance at recovery. But she needed to make it look good. "I'm sorry."

She thrust the stake forward through his chest, just missing his heart.

His eyes widened in shock and pain.

Rose leaned forward, getting close to Max's ear. "Do what you need to. I'm lost."

The undead released him at her command, and he slumped to the ground. The stake stuck out of his unmoving chest. Regret and shame soured her belly.

Rose locked down her feelings and walked to Mistress Yaneli. If Mistress Yaneli suspected Max might still be alive or Joshua was still near, she'd kill them both. Rose had no idea where Daniel had gone. She didn't want him to witness what she'd had to do to Max. She'd delay as much as she could until help could arrive.

"Come, we have a city to introduce ourselves to." Mistress Yaneli nodded at Calder and patted Rose on the shoulder.

Rose followed her.

"Luke? Help Max. Please," Rose sent once she left the clearing.

She could feel Luke and his scouts peel off and circle back. She severed the connection. If Max survived, he would be better off if she didn't know.

Rose had to hope Luke was fresh enough to know to pull the stake from Max's chest. Otherwise, he would die.

26

MAX

<u>Evening, Primum second, 300 years post-Merge</u>

Max felt the stake slide out past his heart. Pain sliced through him. Each breath was an agony. He hadn't expected Rose to act so fast. He'd seen the decision in her face and had understood. He'd known if there was any way she could save him she would. And if she had really wanted him dead, he would be. She must have wanted him to live.

A zombie held the stake in his hands. He looked far fresher than any zombie Max had ever seen.

"I'm Luke. We need to save Rose," the voice in his head said.

The zombie with the stake grunted.

Max tried to move his arm, but agony pierced him. He was going to be useless unless he had a way to heal himself. Daniel would know what to do, but where was Daniel? Max remembered the elixir Daniel had given him. If he was lucky, the bottle was still in his satchel.

"See if the bottle is in my bag," Max sent to Luke.

Luke crouched and fished through Max's satchel. He pulled out a bottle and pulled off the top.

The first drop tingled as it had the first time Rose had given him some. Warmth and energy coursed through his body. The pain faded, replaced by the feeling of his flesh stitching together. He took a deep breath and marveled at the lack of pain.

The bottle still had some liquid left at the bottom. He tucked it inside his satchel.

Rose's words, *I'm lost*, echoed in his head. She had been sane when she'd stabbed him. She had hoped he would live. It had been all she could give him. She thought she was lost, and that Mistress Yaneli still had her children. He was in the woods far away from the town. And Rose was alone among enemies.

The brush rustled to his left, and Joshua stepped out. "I wasn't sure you could survive that."

Relief flooded Max. "Luke helped me."

Joshua nodded at Luke. "Serene went to get help. Not only for the undead army, but for the two rogue wizards. We have to slow them down if we can."

"I don't know how to do that." Max had never felt more useless.

"I have an idea," Luke said.

Max felt a stirring of hope. If they could delay the army, that would give them a chance to remove the magic controlling Rose. "Luke says he has an idea for disrupting the army."

Joshua nodded. "But how do we get Rose to wherever Wren is?"

"I could track them down by scent, but I can't mess with the army and do that at the same time," Max said. He was sure whatever plan Luke had would involve Max getting close to the zombie army.

Joshua nodded thoughtfully. "I could track Wren down, but my body would be helpless." Max remembered how Joshua had seemed distant; had he left his body when checking out the cemetery?

"*I could protect him,*" Luke volunteered.

Max jerked in shock. "*Why would you do that?*" Luke wasn't acting like any zombie he'd known. Of course, movies from Hope and his own two encounters were hardly a good basis for knowing anything about zombies.

"*When Rose is free, she will set us free. This is the best chance at being released,*" Luke said.

Max wondered what 'free' meant to a zombie. Was death freeing to them, or did Luke mean they'd have another chance at life somehow? He hadn't thought zombies could think or speak, let alone volunteer for anything. But the sense he got from Luke was that he was honest about his ability and willingness to help.

Max told Joshua what Luke had said. Joshua thought for a moment and then nodded. "I can't think of anything else that might work."

Max's stomach rebelled, but he knew the only way to stop the army was to stop Rose. She was one of his best friends, and they'd grown up together. He knew how much martial arts training she'd had and how hard she'd trained. "When you talk to Wren, make sure he understands. Rose is ideal for leading an army. She studied martial arts and was a whiz at chess. If she's leading them, they will win."

Joshua nodded, looking grim. He sat with his back against the biggest tree. "I need to get started. Leave Luke here when you go." Joshua turned to Luke. "No snacking."

Luke chuckled.

"*What's the plan for disrupting the army?*" Max asked Luke.

Luke explained what Rose had discovered about controlling a zombie army. "*Put Pauline and Fred in control of the army. It will fall apart in no time. You'll have to talk to them.*" Luke sent a dart of mental energy to Fred.

Max followed and reached out to Fred. He could feel the line of communication he had heard the voices through. *"Want to help me disrupt an army?"*

"Save us," Fred said.

Max realized Fred was much older than Luke, and that very trait was what would help him disrupt the army. *"I will."*

Max felt Fred's willingness to help him. The rest of the zombies joined him. He put the newest in charge and started them walking to catch up with Rose.

"Take care of my friend," Max said to Luke.

Max could hear the voices of the other zombies in his head. Even this far away, he could feel Rose exert her control. She had the zombies organized with some of them acting as information conduits, just as Luke had said she would. *So, she didn't have direct control of each zombie....*

He found one of the zombies in charge of a group of zombies. The newest ones were the most well preserved and seemed to have the clearest voices.

"Help me save Rose," he asked the one with the clearest voice. *"Put Fred in charge."*

The zombie chuckled. Max could feel the zombie reach for Fred and then switch spots. It happened so fast it was almost like magic. Max felt the focus of the zombies shift, as if they had all stopped what they were doing and turned to look toward Fred for instruction. Fred had no instructions to give and was not able to maintain the connection.

Max could feel the moment the line of communication and control splintered, and the zombies wandered away.

A flash of wonder and annoyance flashed through the line as Rose stopped the army and mentally fetched the ones who were wandering. Her stopping was a good sign. He would have guessed she could have kept them walking if she had wanted to.

She must be trying to help delay the army as well. Which meant she wouldn't seek him. Not unless she had to.

While Rose was distracted, Max had the fresh zombie replace the older one in his line, sending many more zombies spinning out of control.

He wasn't sure how long before Mistress Yaneli or Calder would catch on.

Once they did, they would find him and kill him.

27

ROSE

<u>Evening, Primum second, 300 years post-Merge</u>

Rose barely saw the trees around her as she struggled to control the army. Each time a section lost communication with the rest of the mass, she would have to move the unruly undead and put him or her at the end of the line. She knew it was Max who was doing this to her and her army.

Knowing Max was alive after what she had done brought her a small measure of peace. She was both frustrated and glad that Max was delaying her. She could feel Calder and Mistress Yaneli pushing her to force the army forward.

Their control felt like being choked out.

After a long pause, when she pulled Fred from the top spot in the western part of her army and regathered all the zombies, Calder pushed her shoulder.

"What is going on?" Calder snarled.

"The army isn't responding as they should," Rose said. It was true, just not completely accurate.

"Get better control of them," he said. He rolled his eyes as if he shouldn't have to tell her such a thing.

She needed a way to delay Calder's discovery of Max's interference. Fred grunted in her head and she got an idea.

"This is what I am dealing with." She pushed the essence of Fred toward Calder.

Calder commanded Fred to move and the zombie ended up hitting a tree. He hit the tree, got up, and hit the tree once more. It was the tunnel all over again. Rose fought hard to keep her expression and mental energy somber.

"Useless," Calder muttered as he stomped toward Mistress Yaneli.

Rose felt the shift as another old zombie was inserted into the line. The whole right wing of her army wandered away.

She pretended not to notice and focused on getting Fred to stand up. The longer she could delay the army, the better defenses the city would be able to muster. And the more danger she would be in from Calder and Mistress Yaneli.

Calder argued with Mistress Yaneli and wasn't paying attention to Rose. She overheard snatches of 'stupid' and 'zombie,' but not much else.

With any luck, her friends had gotten to safety. She could feel that much of the army had wandered away. Some had even started the process of re-burying themselves because of the coming dawn.

"What's really going on?" Calder snarled. He grabbed the front of her shirt and stared into her eyes. "Why did you lose half my power?"

The control element he had wrapped around her tightened until she could barely breathe.

"Tell me." His face grew red, and he gritted his teeth. The

vessels in his eye popped, leaving a smear of red in his eye. "The whole truth."

She fought the command, trying to figure out a way to twist the meaning of his words so she didn't have to answer. But there was no way to dodge this command. It echoed in her head and with each echo the pressure built. Searing pain exploded in her head. She could feel blood trickle down her lip.

The answer was forced past her unwilling lips. "Max." The pain and pressure lifted immediately, but left a wave of remorse and guilt.

Calder glanced at Mistress Yaneli. She nodded and went back into the woods the way they'd come. Fear for Max and the others squeezed Rose's chest more than the control element. Everyone was in danger because of her.

"Save what you can and keep going. We have to attack before they can rally defenses." Calder poked Rose in the shoulder.

Rose did the best she could and got roughly half of the army marching forward. This smaller army was easier to control.

The strategist in her knew if she shed all of the old zombies it would make the army more responsive. She also knew Calder was watching her more carefully. She wasn't sure if he had studied for war or just wished for power. If it was the latter, she could make huge mistakes and hopefully still save lives.

The thick forest felt like it went on forever, but she could smell the city ahead. Up the next hill the trees parted, bringing them back to the crops. The first zombie broke the tree line, and she used his vision.

Carts and boxes had been placed in front of the fields. From behind the wooden barriers, archers waited, the tops of their bows like bug antennas.

If she were really trying to take over the town, she'd send the oldest zombies out in front as a distraction and take two or three teams of her freshest zombies and circle to the side. The fresh zombies could be stealthy. They could sneak up on the archers or trap the archers between the two forces. If she had enough zombies, she would send some into the streets to sow confusion.

The people she needed to kill to take over would hide if the city was under siege. She'd wait for the fervor to die down and then send in her best zombies to take out the leaders. Then she'd bring in the big showy army of zombies and demand leadership. It would be a quick victory if no one opposed her. Would Calder ask for her opinion on what to do?

Fear clawed at her throat. He could force her to use her plan to take over.

Calder watched her. "What are you waiting for? Attack."

The relief was warm in Rose's chest. The mage hadn't thought a non-mage had any good ideas or, had he put her in the dumb undead category? Whatever the cause, she was grateful for the reprieve. She could go with his plan of "storm the castle."

She sent all of the zombies in for a frontal attack, and then she stepped back to the cover of the trees. The zombies wanted to die, so the arrows and fire that killed them only sent a small twinge to her conscience. But the joy she could feel as they escaped the evil magic which held them to this world eased her mind. She sent a little farewell to each one who perished.

"Why aren't they winning?" Calder gestured frantically to the zombies. He stood tall and paced outside the cover provided by trees and bushes. If she were lucky, an arrow would end his career as a wizard and dictator.

A shot of something mystical streaked past where he had just been. His surprise weakened his hold on her.

He took out a charm and muttered something she couldn't make out. A ball of fire streaked across the field, setting fire to zombies and just missing a cart. He sent two more before he actually hit a box being used as cover.

She backed away. An awareness of Daniel's wild scent, a mixture of wolf and sage, tickled her awareness. Joy quickly turned to fear. *Daniel.* If he came any closer, she might be forced to hurt him. She glanced at Calder, who wasn't paying attention to her.

Daniel's scent lured her. She ducked farther back into the woods. Calder didn't notice, and sent another blast of fire toward the town's archers.

Didn't Daniel know how much danger he would be in if he stayed near her? She'd be forced to kill him. Daniel wouldn't be able to survive the way Max had been able to, because he wasn't an undead. She rubbed at the ache in her chest that sprung up at the thought. She had to follow Daniel and warn him away.

She followed his scent through the trees, but was never quite able to see him. A stream gurgled ahead. He was on the other side of the stream with several others. The scents of feathers, sweat, and oddly enough, cinnamon, were vaguely familiar.

She jumped the stream. Daniel's scent led her toward a glimmer between the trees.

She stepped forward and parted the branches. She wasn't a mage, but she recognized the glimmer was part of a spell circle. It sparkled on the ground and looked like fireflies in a conga line. It was beautiful and probably deadly.

Daniel must have realized she couldn't be saved. The circle was probably magic that would kill her. It was the only thing that made sense. If she were to die, then the army would stop working and the town would survive. Hope would be free. The people she had grown up with and all of the people in the town would be safe. Even Daniel could move on and live his life. A life without her.

The urge to live grabbed her by the throat. She would never see if Mistress Yaneli had saved her children. She would never see Serene and Joshua again. And then there was Daniel.

As if her thoughts of him had called him, he stepped from the brush. "You must come over here." His tone was soft and beguiling. He held out his hand and stood in front of the spell circle.

She hesitated. She wanted to be near him, but didn't want to die. Even if it was necessary.

Something moved at the edge of her vision. Behind Daniel, Mistress Yaneli moved forward, hands raised to cast a spell. Her hard gaze locked on Daniel's back and stirred in Rose an awareness of his vulnerability to Mistress Yaneli's attack. Daniel would die if Rose didn't do something. Adrenaline set her heart racing. She threw herself forward, tackling Daniel and propelling him into the spell circle.

She would protect him with her last breath.

Darkness sparkled and then consumed her.

28

MAX

If Max hadn't been a few paces behind Rose, he never would have seen how fast she had moved to tackle Daniel. Why had—

The ground where Daniel stood exploded. Max flinched.

Mistress Yaneli muttered, "....waste of magic..." from the tree line.

Max realized he had only a moment to react before she cast the next spell. The non-magical kids had learned the gap between spells was the time to get physical, either by running or by grabbing on to the caster and hoping for the best. He had always run.

Rose and Daniel had both landed in the middle of the glittering spell circle. Neither one of them moved. Fear for Rose and Daniel twisted in his gut. They were sitting ducks and made the perfect, unobstructed target for Mistress Yaneli's ire.

He didn't think the lines of the spell circle would protect

against Mistress Yaneli. She'd fry Rose and Daniel and not even feel bad. And then she would move on and pick off anyone else she found, including his friends.

Max only had seconds to decide before the opportunity was lost.

He sprinted across the clearing and grabbed Mistress Yaneli before the next spell could be cast. He felt the fizzle of the wasted magic as a tingle in his arms. She bucked in his grip, but he kept her arms pinned.

"Release me," Mistress Yaneli commanded.

A quiet voice in the back of his mind whispered. *"Mistress Yaneli only wanted what was best for Hope. She wouldn't hurt anyone."* The thoughts repeated, getting slightly more insistent each time.

Max relaxed his grip. He'd never fought before. Why fight now? After all, Mistress Yaneli only wanted what was best.

"Good," she purred. *"Release me."*

The block on his memories of Hope burst. The image of Eleanor on her deathbed rose. She'd been pale and wan as she struggled to breathe. "Mistress Yaneli caused the plague. You must warn the others before it is too late," she'd whispered. Then she died. Her gaze locked on his, and seemed to will him to save the town.

Rage burned through Max's system, and he tightened his grip. The fear sizzled away, leaving him with a startling clarity.

He had to get justice. He looked for something he could use against Mistress Yaneli.

She jerked and struggled, but he held her, fighting to control her arms.

She went still and muttered something under her breath. The tingle of a spell enfolded him again. Too late he realized he should have prevented her from speaking.

Max remembered what Wren had said about emotion

making spells go awry for a wizard. What could he say to piss her off? A picture of young Yaneli's face twisting in jealousy from the vision Ember had shown him flashed into his mind. It had happened when Ember had talked to Calder.

"Your sister was a better wizard than you are." Max made his tone as derisive as possible.

Mistress Yaneli snarled, and the magic fizzled around him, but it wasn't enough. He could still feel the blaze of power just waiting to be released. He needed her to be too angry to use that power.

"Hope would have done anything Ember had wanted without the control spell."

Mistress Yaneli hissed, but the power still swirled around her.

"Glenn loved Ember more than Calder loved you. Especially after what happened to your face." He cringed at the low blow.

She shrieked. Her whole body shook with rage. The feeling of magic distanced, but she bucked her body as if possessed.

Max held on, wondering if he'd been a fool to take on a wizard. If she calmed down enough she would kill him. He had to find something to use to restrain her.

On the other side of the clearing, a loud snap drew his gaze. Calder stormed forward, accompanied by the faint smell of charred fabric and scorched hair. His robe hung in burnt tatters and his hair stood on end. When his gaze landed on Max, Calder's face twisted into a snarl. His eyes blazed with cold fury.

Max wondered how long he could last against two wizards.

29

ROSE

Rose woke up with the taste of grass in her mouth. The sense that something was wrong zipped through her nerve endings. There was an odd burnt smell in the air, and her body felt abnormally loose. She got to her hands and knees amidst the glittering spell circle.

"*Behind you.*" Joshua's voice sounded in her head.

Daniel stirred next to her. "What?"

Rose jerked to look behind her and saw Calder coming out of the woods. His face was twisted in a snarl and spittle dripped from his mouth. His robes flared around him, exposing the glowing necklace. He carried a sword dripping with blood.

Rose climbed to her feet. Her body felt heavy, her movements slow. In this state, Calder had the advantage physically.

Why didn't he cast a spell at her?

"You bitch." He lunged forward with his bloody sword pointed at her.

Rose's training kicked in. She dodged to the side, avoiding the slice of his sword. He'd have to turn his whole body to hit her, where she only had to flick her hand forward.

She ducked and hit Calder with the palm of her hand and then dodged back and to the side again.

Calder spit blood and raised his hand. His expression calmed and hardened. Even though she had no magical talent, magic did affect her. She needed to stop him from casting. Maybe the unchecked rage prevented him from casting spells?

"If you had known anything about armies we could've taken the city," she taunted him.

He snarled, and the magic at his fingertips fizzled. "You won't win that easily, *girl*."

She popped him again. His head snapped back with the force of her blow. She needed to stop him. If she didn't, he would just find another way to create a monster to lead the undead army. She didn't want to be responsible for what he would do to some poor person in the future or to the people in both towns.

He pushed her and she fell back. Calder took a breath and lifted his fingers.

She dodged again and a crack of lightning whizzed from his fingers and thudded into the ground where she had been standing a moment before.

He was gaining control of himself. She looked around for something she could use to stop him. The spell circle was still to her right, still sparkling.

She was free from Calder's control because of that spell circle. She dodged again, the lightning singeing her arm.

She wondered what would happen if she dumped him into the spell circle. Would that cause him pain? Daniel in wolf form darted behind Calder and stopped. Daniel turned his furry head and looked at her.

Calder grinned at her. "You know this is the end for you."

Rose saw the opportunity as Calder stepped toward her. She could trip him. She took a deep breath, and just as the lightning was leaving his fingers, she plowed into him and dumped them both back in the spell circle.

30

MAX

<u>Evening, Primum second, 300 years post-Merge</u>

Max could do nothing as Rose fell into the spell circle and dragged Calder with her. Energy poured out of Calder and the glowing, pulsating necklace around his neck.

Even from here, with Mistress Yaneli struggling in his arms, Max could feel the magical power sizzle. He'd seen spells overload before, with disastrous results.

"Noooo. The soul-bond. Calder!" Mistress Yaneli went crazy, biting and scratching and kicking him. She jerked, suddenly far stronger than any human woman should be. She broke his grip and launched herself into the spell circle.

The energy in the circle pulsed and the original fireflies vanished. Valeria and Wren ran into the clearing to each end of the circle and stood just outside of the writhing layer of energy. The look on Wren's face said they were all going to die.

"Wren, remember what we practiced for your sister?" Valeria shouted.

Wren nodded calmly. They both chanted and danced. They were not dancing the same dance, but something wild and deep.

Valeria's arms weaved in a sinuous and complicated pattern as her body swayed to some internal beat. Wren's wings were out, and he used them to execute flips and rolls that would have won a gold medal in the old world. All the while they both chanted the same words.

Max could feel the uncontrolled energy surging. Fear gripped him. He wished he could do something, anything, to help contain the power.

Mistress Yaneli screamed. The added power sent a shock wave through the clearing and knocked Max off his feet.

His vision darkened to almost black. The sounds around him faded. Slowly his sight returned and silence lay heavy around him. What had happened?

He sat up. The air still vibrated with a low-level power, but most of the energy seemed to be trapped by the slight pulsing that came from within the spell circle where he had last seen Rose. He dreaded casting his eyes to the spell circle. He didn't want to see Rose and his other friends dead. With a deep breath, he forced his gaze to the circle.

Skeletal remains locked in an embrace smoldered in the center of what had been the spell circle. They each wore a necklace that still glowed with unearthly power. The bigger skeleton had burnt robes and a bloody sword near his left side. The smaller skeleton had a fragment of white handkerchief clutched in one hand. The skeletons must be Calder and Mistress Yaneli locked in an eternal embrace.

He stepped closer to the bodies.

Daniel was on his knees next to Rose just outside of the spell circle. He wore the stoic face Max had seen so many times. He checked her pulse and ripped open his bag. The stab of his hand through his hair said what he needed wasn't there.

A feeling of hopelessness weighed Max down. If Daniel couldn't help Rose, then no one could. If only there was something he could do. He didn't know anything about healing and anyway, Rose was an undead. The idea exploded in his mind—she was an undead like Max was—which meant the potion he had saved would save her.

Max fumbled to move his satchel to access the pocket. He opened his bag. The potion was unbroken. "I have one."

He scrambled to pull Rose closer and popped the stopper out with his teeth.

The half dose swirled as he brought it to her lips. The potion dribbled into her mouth. He held his breath. Was he too late? Was it enough?

Her face pinkened, and she took a deep breath. Joy suffused him. He hugged her to him, laughing and crying at the same time. They'd done it. Hope was free. Rose could go back to her children. Eleanor was still dead. Grief brought an ache to his chest and a heaviness to his body, but he had friends, like Daniel, who would help him through it.

Daniel sat back on his haunches and watched Rose. The expression on his face was unreadable. But Max swore he looked sad.

Which made no sense to Max. They had saved Rose. It was obvious Daniel cared about her. Based on the set of his shoulders, Daniel probably thought Max was Rose's love from the past. And being a man of honor, he would not interfere if Rose loved him.

Damn it.

Wren parted the bushes, and Valeria stumbled out first, leaving a trail of twigs and leaves. Wren caught her before she could fall. They huddled together and seemed to hold each other upright.

"You guys okay?" Max asked.

Wren and Valeria jerked and turned to face them. At first Max thought Wren and Valeria were blushing because of their embrace, but the color didn't fade as they approached. A smudge of dirt painted Valeria's left cheek, and she had leaves in her hair.

"This is normal after a big spell." Wren's voice croaked.

Valeria nodded and winced. She moved her neck slowly.

The power of the spell must have thrown them into the woods.

"Is everyone okay?" Wren glanced around the group. When his gaze landed on him, Max nodded.

Daniel muttered, "Yes," without looking up.

"It's a good thing I pulled my wings in. That would have broken them." Wren brushed some twigs off his feathers and rolled his shoulders.

"You just needed to land in a nice, soft pile of leaves." Valeria patted her hair but didn't look as if she had been thrown through the bushes.

Wren scowled at her and then grinned. "After all that, did you use magic to break your fall? That's amazing."

Valeria grinned at him and then turned to look at the spell circle. "We set the spell to break any bonds on a person who entered the circle. There's always energy when breaking bonds. We hadn't expected that much energy. They must have had a bond to the shield as well as to each other."

"We felt the shield come down, but there was no extra energy in the world at large," Wren said.

"They must have put the energy into the necklaces." Max pointed at the glowing stones.

Valeria picked her way into the circle and used a handkerchief to pull the necklaces off of what was left of Mistress Yaneli and Calder.

"What will you do with them?" Wren asked.

"Maybe they should go to the archive." Valeria tucked them into her bag. Max couldn't tell if she was serious. From the look Wren gave Valeria, Max doubted the necklaces would make it to the archive right away.

Rose stirred in his arms. Max looked down at her as her eyes fluttered open, and a small flash of dismay in her expression was quickly replaced with joy. "You're still alive."

"Still kicking." Max helped her sit up.

"What happened?" Rose looked dazed.

"The spell circle broke their control over you," Max said.

Valeria came and sat beside Rose. "Yes, we used what we learned about Max to construct a spell circle which would remove their control. We had to make some changes, so we weren't in the circle. Seemed like a wise move, since you may have tried to kill us." Valeria winked at Rose.

Rose's smile faltered. "The bond was so tight. I did what I could to help you save the town. I had to stab Max and lead the army. But I stabbed Max in a place he would recover from. And I didn't tell Calder the plan that would have taken the city," she whispered.

Max had no doubt that if Rose had wanted to, she would have control of the city, and Calder and Mistress Yaneli would now be the rulers of both towns.

Wren smiled at her. "You did good. I know you could have won. Joshua says you were the only one who could beat him at chess."

Valeria touched Daniel's arm. "Are you okay? The spell circle would have broken any sort of bond. Even pack bonds."

Daniel smiled sadly. "I have no bonds to break. I should go

see if there are any wounded people in town." He left the clearing quickly without glancing back.

Rose stared after him. A look of disappointment swept her features. "We need to keep the promise to the zombies." She rubbed her forehead and glanced at Max before dropping her gaze to the ground.

Max offered Rose his hand. Instead of the quick leap up he had expected of Rose, he had to pull her to her feet. She must be exhausted.

She didn't say anything, but the distance in her expression told him everything he needed to know. Rose was having an argument with herself. He could guess she was struggling with herself about her feelings for Daniel and what to do about them.

"If he knows you're interested in him, he would admit he's interested in you," Max said.

Rose laughed with a sound both freer and lighter than she had for a long time. "I'm that transparent?"

Max grinned. "Yup. Go get your man."

EPILOGUE - ROSE

<u>Afternoon, Primum third, 300 years post-Merge</u>

Rose took a deep breath to steady her nerves and glanced at the man walking next to her. Daniel had agreed to come with her to Hope to help with the aftermath of the plague.

Her memories of Hope were still twisted and unclear. Max had told her that her children hadn't been dead when he had left Hope after her departure. Ferrik had hidden them. He had truly done what he could as he'd promised. The thought brought a crash of emotions to her chest. Part of her believed her girls were dead, and she didn't want false hope.

But, she couldn't help picturing them five years older and looking like their dad. Her chest ached. If she didn't go to Hope, then she wouldn't have to deal with finding out they'd succumbed to the plague or any number of terrible things that could have happened in five years. Or that Max's memory of her daughters had been manipulated, like so many of his other memories.

And then there was the issue that she wasn't alive any longer. Did she have any place in their world now that she was the living dead?

She wanted Daniel's support, even though she was unsure of his feelings toward her. He was still a good friend.

So, she wrapped up what she could before facing her daughter's fates. It had been less than twenty-four hours since the shield around Hope had come down, and she'd had a series of surprises.

She kept her promise to the undead and freed them, except for Luke and a small squad of newly undead who decided they wanted to live. After the help Luke had given Max and Joshua, she'd felt she owed them. She had a small worry about what they might be up to, but she would worry about that later.

Valeria and Wren had taken her aside and told her how much Daniel worried about her and worked to help her. If not for Daniel's insistence, they wouldn't have set up the spell circle and gotten her free from the control spell. That had to be proof he cared.

Wren also informed her with some glee that Max had made promises to help him with his sister. Whatever was going on there was bound to be intense. She'd help Max however she could when the time came.

The sunlight blinded her for a moment and distracted her from her thoughts. A few steps away was where the shield had been.

She slowed. Dread rolled in her belly and sent a sour taste to her mouth. She couldn't face her life if her kids were really dead.

She glanced at Daniel again. He didn't look at her. During the walk through the town and the woods, Daniel hadn't given her any of his shy smiles. He hadn't said anything at all.

He was not talkative, but his behavior seemed odd for him.

Instead of guessing what was going on with him, she'd decided to ask him. "Are you sure you are up to this?"

"Yes." He glanced at her before looking away quickly.

She couldn't read his expression. But the 'yes' felt off or forced. His response didn't actually answer the question she really wanted answered. Did he want to be with her?

Rose bit her lip. Maybe her friends were wrong about Daniel. Maybe she had imagined that he might share the same attraction she had to him. When they had been trapped in his house, even with him so sick, he'd made her favorite tea. They had laughed about silly things together. When she had been worried about Serene and Joshua, he eased her fears with a gentle touch. Maybe those things were him just being a great healer. "I know you feel obligated to help anyone who is ill."

He stopped and faced her. "Do you want me to come with you?" He still wore his stoic expression, which made it hard to tell what he was thinking.

"Yes." Rose still wanted to spend time with him. He made her feel safe and loved. She wanted to face the uncertainty of what she would find at Hope with him by her side.

He looked down at the ground and then closed his eyes. And then as if steeling himself, he opened them again. "And why do you want me to come?"

Rose swallowed. In the face of his question and with his lack of response, was she willing to risk telling him? If she didn't tell him, she might never know how he felt. If she told him, then she was vulnerable to his scorn. Though, when she stopped to think about it, she knew he wouldn't treat her with scorn. He was too kind for that. But the fear of rejection was still there. She felt jittery. She would never again meet anyone like Daniel. She had to tell him the truth. "Because I want to spend more time with you."

He seemed to examine her face, and then he grinned at her with his shy smile. "There are many people I could help in the city. I am helping this set of sick people because they're important to you. I want to be with you."

His fond expression shocked her. She had never seen so much emotion on his face. "But I'm undead. You can't..."

Daniel chuckled. "I have a surprise for you. Max and I thought this might help."

"What—"

"Mom! It's mom!" A young voice called out from the direction of Hope.

Running up the gentle hill were two slender girls with curly brown hair wild around their faces. Ferrik walked behind them and waved.

Rose froze for a moment in shock. *My girls are alive!*

She ran and embraced them. All of her fears seemed so silly now that she could feel them in her arms. They laughed and squealed. Her throat was so clogged with emotions she couldn't do anything but hold them.

She glanced up at Daniel and even through her tears could see him smiling.

Once she could speak again, she said, "Girls, I have someone I'd like you to meet."

Even as she turned to introduce Daniel to her girls, she couldn't help but wonder what was going on between Wren and Valeria.

THE END

CONGRATULATIONS ON REACHING the end of Rose's journey! Stay tuned for a sneak peek of the first chapter in the next installment of the Merged Series: "Feather of Prophecy." Find out what Wren and Valeria are hiding.

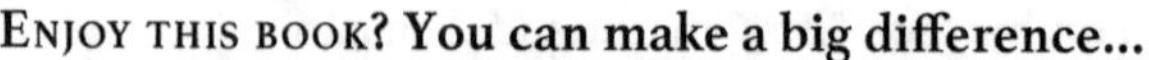

ENJOY THIS BOOK? You can make a big difference...

Reviews are the most powerful tools when it comes to getting notice for my books.

If you enjoyed this book, I'd be so grateful if you'd spend just five minutes leaving a review (as short as you like!).

Thank you very much.

Eager for exclusive content? Want to be the first to know about upcoming releases and get a free short story?

Sign up for Claudia Blood's Newsletter at https://dl.bookfunnel.com/u5nf3wa84m

You can unsubscribe at any time.

BOOK 3: FEATHER OF PROPHECY

Excerpt from Chapter 1: Wren

Pride and excitement made Wren fluff his feathers. His father trusted him to protect himself and his sister on a trip to the West Market. He'd never been given this responsibility or freedom. He'd never been allowed to venture down from their mountain home into New Nadezhda by himself and being able to take Alesia, his cosseted twin, conferred a high honor.

"Look!" Alesia danced on her toes, but managed to keep her cloak tucked around her. She pointed to a building on the corner. The bright light sparkled on the dew on the cobblestones, making everything seem new. The smell of honeyed cookies wafted to Wren from the open door.

He smiled at his sister. "Let's get one."

They entered the shop and the bell jangled. A human used a long wooden paddle to pull the breakfast treats out of the oven. The smell of baked bread and honey with cinnamon filled the room.

"Oh, can we have one?" Alesia whispered and gripped his arm.

He patted her hand and said to the baker. "May we have two, please?"

The man turned with a soft whirr and metal ping, and smiled. "Of course, Prince." Wren recognized him as someone his father had aided. The whir and the ping was the clever mechanism on the man's left foot which helped him walk. The Aero's artisans had built the device on his father's orders.

The human took the two honey cakes and placed them in the eating pouch and handed them to Wren.

Wren fished out a few coins and put them on the counter. "Thank you."

"No charge." The man crossed his arms.

"Please, take the money." Alesia's voice was soft and full of entreaty.

The man stared at her for a moment and then loosened his arms and nodded. "Yes, Princess."

Wren would not have been able to resist her request and was not surprised that the human had been unable to as well. There was something about his sister that made people want to aid her.

Wren and Alesia left, each holding their treat. The honey tasted like sunshine and reminded him of an early morning song.

"Can we try that?" Alesia was already done with her treat. She pointed to a shop labeled. 'Fortune Teller'.

Wren shivered. His family already had a curse and a prophecy handed down in the royal family. *'Two halves united shall burn and be reborn.'*

The last thing he or his family needed was another prophecy. No one knew what the first one meant. The fact that two members of his family had died by fire just added to his unease.

The fortune teller shop was different from the others on the street, exuding a sense of foreboding. He had not been to the city often, and Wren had never noticed the shop before.

He glanced at his sister to say no. But saw her excitement clearly written on her face. Her wide smile and sparkling eyes begged him to say yes. He hesitated. Keeping his sister safe was the most important thing to him. A close second was her happiness.

She was just as adept at reading Wren's expression because she said, "Oh come on Wren, how much danger can we be in? Dad sent guards to watch over us." She waved her hand at the nearby roof.

One of his father's guards sat on the roof watching them. How had he missed the sun glinting off that much armor?

The feeling of independence and trust disappeared. Frustration and anger roiled in his gut. He clenched his teeth til they ached. Instead of telling her no, which was probably the right thing, he took her hand and led her to the shop.

The door opened with a groan that sent a shiver down his spine. He'd taken enough of his apprentice training to feel the press of magic in the room. The small entry opened into a large room. Most of the magic emanated from something covered in the middle of the wooden table in the far corner. Drapes hung not only on the windows making the interior dim, but nearby that looked like they could be closed for privacy.

The magic didn't seem to be malicious, at least not yet. But he got the impression that the magic watched him and his sister. He didn't like the feel of the magical gaze upon her, so he turned to go.

"Welcome to Madam Red's shop." The voice came from a dark corner on his left side.

A woman stepped from the shadows. She looked like a human, but something about her aura said she was anything but. Curly, red hair spilled across her shoulder and blended into red, layered silk. The different red colors in her garb gave the illusion that flames hovered around her.

Wren backed his sister toward the door.

"I am not here to harm you. I can clearly see your futures," the woman said softly.

"I want to know." Alesia sang and pulsed forward. Her face was bright and excited.

The kind smile that the woman gave Alesia convinced him to stay. Divination magic was not the easiest to control. If a person was good at such magic, they could give a hint to the future. If they were bad at that type of magic or unlucky, they might as well make up the future for how accurate the fortune would be.

"Are you Madam Red?" Wren glanced around the dim interior and then focused on the woman.

"I am, young prince." The woman gave him a polite smile. "Come sit here." She led them to a small round table in the corner. She pulled out a chair and gestured to Alesia to sit. When Alesia did, Madam Red invited Wren to sit too.

He moved to the table and sat at the edge of the chair.

Madam Red removed a cloth from a fisted-sized, red crystal. The light sparkled on the gem's surface. Under the surface, white and red clouds rolled past.

The magic strengthened and the otherness and power puffed the feathers between his shoulders. He glanced at his sister to see if she could feel the magic.

She sat frozen and stared into the gem. Her blue eyes wide and her goofy and excited smile beamed from her lips. The smile she had used when they had found a minecart and decided to take it through the mountain. Luckily when the ride ended with them launching off the rails and into the cavern, their wings had saved them.

Madam Red cleared her throat. She had sat at the table across from them while he was distracted.

"What's wrong with my sister?" Wren froze as Madam Red's eyes shifted from brown to bright blue. "You are the only one who can right this wrong and save her."

Wren's throat suddenly went dry. This was a test. There were always tests. He swallowed and pushed down his fear. "What must I do?"

She smiled. "There is a prophecy for you. And a word of advice."

Wren nodded. He knew he would have to memorize the prophecy as the words would never be repeated. As soon as he could, he would have to write the words down so the prophecy could be put in the chronicle.

Her gaze lifted to the ceiling. She shivered and her silk garb flickered around her like flames.

Son and daughter of the saviors of fenix
Time runs out to repair
that which was sundered after the Merge
Isolate the pair until first light on her day of birth
Seek the kept flame and release
Two halves united shall burn and be reborn.
Only a bound witch can save them all
Or the immortal shall die
and break open fully the portal to the abyss

Wren repeated the words in his head a few times, adding them to his memory. The middle part he'd already known. The fact that this seemed related to a prophesy long held in his family sent a shiver down his spine. He'd been told about the prophecy his whole life.

Wren reviewed the parts. He'd look up fenix and see if he could find the reference. The Merge was when the human realm and his own realm came together in a sudden violent event. After three hundred years, no one was sure what had caused the Merge, only that the event had decimated populations and forced the magical people and humans to live together.

He had no idea who the pair could be, unless that was another reference to son and daughter. There were many ways to bind a person, but to bind a witch implied a connection that was magical. Nothing else in the new words made any sense.

Madam Red sat motionless with her hands serenely on her lap. She gazed at Alesia who gazed back at her and then they both turned to face Wren. Alesia's eyes were iridescent. The weight of the air was different as if a storm approached. He struggled to breath with the heaviness on his chest. Whatever had possessed their grandmother and ruined her life, now had a hold of his sister.

"It must be done by her 30th birthday or all is lost." Alesia blinked her eyes and they returned to their natural blue. The spirit finding Alesia was his fault. His throat thickened and his stomach churned.

"What is your word of advice?" Wren asked, forcing the words past the constriction.

"Run, the demons are here."

MARKED BY CLAUDIA BLOOD

Searching for her lost sister, she uncovers a terrible secret—one that could cost her everything...

Valeria uncovers a dark secret that could save her and reunite her with the one she loves. But she soon realizes that the demons she's up against will stop at nothing to keep her from finding the truth.

Set in a world where ancient family secrets hold immense power, Marked is a heart-pounding standalone Novelette in the Merged Series.

With her loved ones under the control of ruthless enemies, Valeria must navigate a treacherous family feud that could ultimately cost her everything.

Read if you you love intense family dynamics, huge family secrets, and gripping action.

This is the origin story for Valeria. Find out how she got her tattoos.

Read Now!

ACKNOWLEDGMENTS

Thanks to my hubby and family who allow me to wander away when I need to write.

To my VA Kelly I can't thank you enough for your undying enthusiasm and design sense. Social media is way less scary with you on my side.

To my amazing developmental editor Dawn Alexander who helped me organize my chaos and keep my inner achiever from getting too enthusiastic.

Thank you Fenley Grant for your amazing editing skills and for working me in when I am inevitably late.

Thank you Wendy for reading and giving feedback to my writing since college. (A scary number of years ago) You were always able to find a nugget of good that kept me going.

Thank you to the ladies at Lakehouse Writers group, Tammy, Val, MaryAnna, B, Jay, and Kim who have been a constant source of inspiration, motivation, and sanity checking.

Thank you to Val and MaryAnna who kept me honest on our accountability texts and for helping me figure out the end of this book. You both were so patient with my what-if-ing.

Thank you Antha and Christine for the many, many, many writing sprints. Without you guys I never would have gotten the book done.

Thank you to Calley for the daily checkins. Cookies!

ABOUT THE AUTHOR

Claudia Blood writes mystical realms and futuristic worlds, where underdogs defy authority, defeat demons, and discover their destined family amidst the chaos.

Her love of Epic Fantasies led her from life as a research scientist right into that of an award-winning author. With works such as the Renegades Rising, *Relic trilogy*, <u>Merged series</u>, and the <u>Supernatural Detective Agency</u>. <u>Claudia Blood</u>'s works cover a wide range of genres and themes that have captivated many.

Juggling her roles as a wife, mom, business analyst, and pet wrangler doesn't leave much free time, but what Claudia has is filled to the brim with creating sci-fi and fantasy novels set in worlds that may be slightly familiar and some that are totally unique and new. Taking inspiration from all kinds of media from *Dungeons & Dragons*, *The Dresden Files*, Alan Dean Foster, and so much more, Claudia Blood crafts stories that entice and keep the reader wondering what will happen next.

For her latest release, visit her at
<u>www.ClaudiaBlood.com</u>

www.ingramcontent.com/pod-product-compliance
Lightning Source LLC
Chambersburg PA
CBHW061236210726
48293CB00003B/792